Cruise Ship Chronicles
Cozy Mystery Series
Book 3

Hope Callaghan

www.hopecallaghan.com
Copyright © 2015
All rights reserved.

Visit my website for new releases and special offers: www.HopeCallaghan.com

A special **thank you** to **Wanda Downs** and **Peggy Hyndman** for taking the time to read and review the third book in my series, Cruise Ship Chronicles, *Lethal Lobster,* and offering all of the helpful advice!

***

I would also like to thank ***Bobby Walters*** for graciously allowing me to use his artwork in *Lethal Lobster.* I happened to stumble upon his work while vacationing in Oceans Springs, Mississippi and discovered his painting *Maine Lobster* would be a perfect fit for this book.

His work is exceptional and I am excited he has offered to allow me to use some of his other works in my upcoming books! ***You can find Bobby and view his art by typing the website below.***

Bobby Walters Fine Art, Hattiesburg, MS

http://bobby-walters.artistwebsites.com/index.html

Table of Contents

[This page left intentionally blank]

Chapter 1

"Therefore do not worry about tomorrow, for tomorrow will worry about itself. Each day has enough trouble of its own." Matthew 6:34 NIV

Millie Sanders trudged up the stairs, her stun gun / flashlight combo clenched tightly in her fist. Her boss, Cruise Director, Andy Walker, had asked her to meet him outside the fitness center and to bring the Taser he had given her as a gift when she first joined the cruise line as assistant cruise director. Although "asked" might be an understatement, at least in Millie's mind. It had been more like a command that she meet him at the fitness center.

Millie, who, at one time, owned a detective agency in West Michigan with her now ex-husband, Roger, had recently managed to end up right in the middle of a couple murder investigations on board the ship.

The last one had been a doozy and now Millie wasn't sure if he really meant to help her by showing her how, exactly, to use a Taser when confronted– or if it was some sort of cruel and unusual punishment to deter her from sticking her nose where it didn't belong.

Millie paused at the top of the stairs. If Andy thought this would stop her from solving crimes and keeping the crew safe, then he was sadly mistaken! That might stop a normal civilian, but not Millie Sanders!

She squared her shoulders, tucked a stray strand of long silver hair behind her ear and reached for the door handle that connected the hall and the workout area.

The area would not open for passenger use for another hour, so if there was any consolation in the whole exercise, her "lesson" would last sixty minutes, tops.

When Millie stepped inside the room, her heart sank. There had to be twenty other crewmembers milling about. Andy was smack dab in the center of the crowd.

Despite the gravity of the situation, Millie almost burst out laughing at the sight of her boss. He was wearing a pair of what looked like plaid pajama bottoms and a wife beater tank top. Tufts of bright red chest hair protruded out the sides of the tattered shirt.

She looked down at her own outfit and the smile disappeared. Hers wasn't much better – a pair of jogging shorts that her friend, Annette Delacroix, had loaned her and a t-shirt from the gift shop that Cat, her other friend, had donated for the cause.

Andy waved her over and motioned her to follow him.

The two of them wandered up the side steps and into a boxing ring that filled one whole section of the workout room. Millie had never noticed it before.

"I'll take that." Andy reached for her Taser.

3

Millie held it out, but for some reason, her hand refused to release its grip and the two of them tugged back and forth for several seconds.

"Let go!" Andy hissed.

Finally, Millie reluctantly released her grip on the flashlight / stun gun combo and took a step back.

The crowd gathered around the ring. Andy turned to address the occupants. "I know you are all here for a demonstration on how to use a stun gun." He pointed to Millie. "My sidekick, Millie, who is also the Assistant Cruise Director, has graciously offered to be my guinea pig."

Millie eyes flew open and her mouth dropped. She most definitely had not volunteered!

Andy patted her back and continued his little speech. "You should never use a stun gun unless you feel that physical harm or bodily injury is imminent."

He shifted the stun gun in his hand and pressed the button. *BUZZ...ZAP!* The sound of pure electricity filled the air.

Next, he placed the Taser side of the weapon against Millie's right arm. Millie's mouth went dry. Her knees grew weak. She scrunched her eyes shut, waiting for the jolt of electricity to pierce her body.

Millie clenched her fists. She drew in a sharp breath and squeezed her eyes shut.

Click! Nothing. Nada. No jolt.

Andy pulled the Taser back. "Always keep the safety lock in place when not in use."

He turned the weapon to the side so the audience could see the lock.

Andy tapped the tip of the Taser on Millie's bare arm.

Tap. Heart attack.

Tap. Another heart attack.

"The arm is not the best area of the body to effectively use a Taser," he told the group.

In one swift movement, Andy lifted the Taser and pressed it against her lips! "This is a much more effective spot!" he announced.

Millie's eyes flew open, a look of sheer terror on her face. She thought she was going to pass out. She tried to say something but the Taser was like searing metal against her lips.

Andy pulled the Taser away from her lips and Millie let out an audible sigh.

"The best places to use a stun gun are areas of the body that contain the most nerve endings."

Andy touched the stun gun under her chin, then the side of her face and stopped when he stuck the gun directly on her eye!

Millie began to sway as the blood drained from her face, certain that this was the ultimate revenge. Andy was going to zap her eye! She would probably go blind.

Andy could see he was getting Millie good. He released his grip on her arm, winked at her and lowered the Taser. "Thank you, Millie for helping me with this demonstration."

Millie darted out of the ring, her legs wobbling as if they were going to abandon her at any moment. She grabbed the railing and scrambled to solid ground.

Andy waited until she was safely out of the ring. "Now I'll demonstrate what actually happens when someone is tased. Brody, c'mon up here."

Brody was the bouncer from the nightclub and he bounded up the steps. He was a big dude with a thick, muscular frame, as if he worked out on a regular basis. Or maybe he was an ex-Marine.

Andy slapped him on the shoulder. "Brody has agreed to allow me tase him, to show you the body's reaction to being zapped by a Taser."

He turned to face Brody. "You sure you're ready for this?"

Brody nodded. A muscle in his jaw tightened. "Can't wait."

The crowd tittered.

Millie rolled her eyes. Brody had to be missing a few marbles!

"What is going on?" Annette had come to stand next to Millie. Cat was behind her. "We heard something about Andy using the Taser on you," she whispered.

"No, he didn't," Millie answered, "but he sure did scare the dickens out of me!"

Andy started to talk. "Now, for the Taser to be most-effective, you have to press it against the body for a full five seconds and hold it there."

Andy lifted the end of the Taser and placed it against Brody's ribcage. "However, I am not going to hold it against Brody's body for the full five seconds, but just for a brief moment so you can see how a person reacts."

Andy looked up. "Ready?"

8

Brody nodded solemnly. "As I'll ever be."

Millie sucked in a breath.

Annette gasped.

Cat's hand flew to her mouth. "Oh my goodness!"

Z-Zap!!

Brody's body stiffened straight out. He jerked back and pulled away from the stun gun. He clutched at his chest and gasped for air, taking quick, shallow breaths.

Andy reached for his arm to steady him. "You alright?"

Brody took a few more shallow breaths, pounded his chest with his fist and shook his head, as if to clear it. "Man that was a trip!"

Millie closed her eyes. "Thank you, God, for sparing me."

Certain that Brody was okay, Andy faced the group. "I need one more volunteer for a quick demonstration," he said.

Millie shrank back. No way was she going up there again!

Andy's eyes scanned the crowd. "Cat!" He waved an arm. "C'mon up!"

Cat shook her head "no" but several crewmembers clapped in encouragement. Finally, Cat caved and slowly wandered across the room and up the steps.

She stood next to Andy, who waited for her in the center of the ring.

"With the ladies, you don't need to use as much power to zap them so I recommend using the lowest setting possible."

He turned to Cat. "Could you please lift your arms up above your head?" he asked.

Cat's eyes widened. Her mouth formed an "O" but nothing came out. Reluctantly, she complied.

The long sleeves of her puffy, pink blouse fell as she lifted her arms. Her shirt edged up slightly, just enough to catch a glimpse of her midriff.

Andy continued to explain the difference between tasing a man and woman but Millie wasn't listening. She was gaping at the long, angry scar that ran from Cat's left side and slashed across her abdomen before it disappeared on the other side.

Millie cupped her hands and whispered in Annette's ear. "Oh my gosh! Look at Cat's scar."

Annette nodded. "That looks wicked."

Millie could not agree more. "I wonder what happened."

"I asked Cat one time, when I noticed it a while back and she clammed up. Whatever happened, she does not want to talk about it," Annette warned.

Millie nodded. Although she was more than a bit curious about whatever happened to Cat that caused such a savage scar, it might bring up painful memories of some accident Cat wanted to forget.

Cat let her arms down and Andy thanked her for her time.

She returned to her spot next to the girls and wiped a hand across her brow. "Whew! That was a close call," she joked.

Andy finished by explaining the different stun guns and prices. He also told them that he had a friend in Miami who owned a personal safety company and that he could get the crew a discount if anyone was interested.

Brody, who was still standing next to Andy in the ring, reached over and jerked the gun / flashlight from Andy's hand. In one swift movement, he jabbed the end on Andy's exposed neck and pulled the trigger.

Millie watched in horror as Andy's eyes widened and then rolled back in his head. His body grew limp. He hit the ground with a loud *thud.*

Brody, unconcerned that Andy was now lying unconscious on the ground, flipped the safety switch and set the gun on the floor before he turned his attention to Andy.

He bent down and shook his shoulder. "Hey big guy. You okay?"

Andy's eyes fluttered. His body jerked. It was as if he was having an aftershock.

Millie darted through the crowd and up the steps. She dropped to her knees and leaned over Andy's still body, certain he was near death. "Andy! Andy! Talk to me!" She tugged on his hand.

All of the sudden, Andy's eyes flew open. He reached up, circled both hands around Brody's throat and started to squeeze. "You could have killed me," he growled.

Millie flung her elbow against Andy's arms, desperate to break the death grip Andy had on poor Brody's throat.

Finally, Andy released his hold.

Brody rubbed his neck. "Sorry boss." He seemed genuinely remorseful, which pacified Andy, at least for the moment.

Millie grabbed Brody's arm and tugged. "We better get out of here before he changes his mind and goes after you again."

Millie kept a close eye on Andy as she and Brody exited the ring.

Several of the employees, including Annette and Cat, wandered into the ring to pick up one of the fliers from the Miami gun shop.

Millie waited at the bottom.

Annette waved the flier in her hand. "I am going to get one of these next time we dock in Miami," she vowed.

Cat stared at the flyer then turned it over to study the other side. "Me, too. You never can be too careful these days."

Millie motioned her friends off to the side, out of the stream of traffic. It had been several days since she'd had a chance to chat with them. The only time she'd seen either one of them was briefly, during Sunday morning chapel.

Millie's ship life had finally settled down and fallen into a regular routine with nary a dead body popping up anywhere.

Cat spoke what Millie had been thinking. "I miss hanging out with you guys. We need to plan to eat together or something..." she trailed off.

Annette opened her mouth to reply when her radio went off. "Annette! You there?"

It was Amit, Annette's right hand man in the kitchen.

Annette plucked the radio from her belt and held it to her lips. "Yeah, Amit. I'm here!"

"We got another FP," he blurted out.

The color drained from Annette's face. "You're kidding."

"I wish I was, Miss Annette," came Amit's somber reply.

"What is FP?" Millie had never heard that term used on the ship.

Annette leaned in. "Food poisoning and this is the second one in less than 24 hours."

Chapter 2

Annette darted out of the fitness center and made a mad dash for the kitchen. Cat and Millie were hot on her heels.

Annette was fast - faster than Millie could have imagined. She left them in the dust.

When they got to the door that led into the kitchen, Millie peeked in the porthole window. She could see Annette and Amit off to one side, their heads close together. Amit had a frown on his face and he was shaking his head.

Millie slowly pushed the door open and tiptoed in. Cat stepped on her heel.

"Ouch!"

"Shhh." Cat shushed her.

Annette clenched her hands in two tight fists and shook them in the air. "I just don't understand! I tasted the lobster bisque before it left this kitchen and *I* didn't get sick!"

Amit shrugged his shoulders, at a loss for words. He was just as bewildered as she was.

Millie came in behind them. "The dish came from this kitchen?" There was always the off chance it had come from somewhere else, like the deli station or specialty dining room.

Annette whirled around. Her face was beet red. She took a quick breath. "Yes, and I don't know how. I tried the dish myself and then sent it down to the officer's dining room. It was supposed to be a special treat," she added.

Annette's eyes began to water. "Anyways, Amit just told me that Captain Vitale was the only one who tried the lobster bisque. Not long after, he became violently ill. He's in his cabin puking his guts out."

Amit nodded. "He is very sick."

Annette wrung her hands. "I'm toast," she groaned. Before Cat or Millie could answer, she turned on her heel and stalked out of the kitchen.

Millie started after her.

Cat reached out and grabbed Millie's arms. "No. Don't go. Let her be. She needs time to vent and nothing we can say right now will help."

Cat had a point. When Millie was upset, she needed to be alone, to mull it over, and maybe even throw a few things...

"You're right," Millie agreed. She turned to Amit, who stared at the door where Annette had just departed.

"Do you think someone is trying to sabotage poor Annette? I mean, it doesn't make any sense that she tasted the dish, sent it down to the officer's dining room and the same dish she sampled made Captain Vitale ill."

Amit nodded. "Yes, Miss Millie. Even I tried it, just to make sure."

He pointed to his chest. "See? I am fine, too."

"Who took the dish down to the dining room?" Cat asked. Perhaps they needed to have a chat with the last person to handle the dish before it arrived in the dining room.

Amit shook his head. "It wasn't me."

Cat and Millie wandered out of the galley. Millie glanced down at her watch. "I have to report to work in 30 minutes and still need to shower and change."

She looked up at Cat. "I'll stop by the gift shop when my shift ends. Maybe we can talk to Annette after that."

Cat worked at Ocean Treasures, the ship's largest gift shop. The shop closed at ten p.m., which would give Millie a chance to return Scout, Captain Armati's teacup Yorkie and Millie's sidekick, back to Captain Armati before meeting up with the girls.

Millie left Cat in the corridor as she picked up the pace and headed to the stairs. She flew down the steps in record time and was in front of her cabin in no time flat.

Sarah, Millie's cabin mate, was nowhere in sight when Millie entered the room.

Millie made a beeline for the bathroom and flung the shower curtain open. She wiggled out of her sweaty clothes and slipped under the warm, cascading water.

Millie had to admit that the Taser demonstration had been helpful. She was surprised at how many of the crew showed up to watch Andy in action. She was thankful that Andy hadn't tased her, especially after having seen what happened to Brody after he was shocked, not to mention Andy when Brody turned the tables.

She made a mental note to ask him exactly what it felt like, just in case she had to use it on someone, somewhere down the road. The ship was full of nefarious activities and Millie had heard tidbits of recent drug busts.

She knew enough from her ex-husband, Roger's, detective business that where there were drugs, there were some shady types lurking around, which reminded her of her poor friend, Annette.

Something fishy was going on. She knew there was no way Annette would be careless with food preparation and she certainly would never send contaminated food down to the officer's dining room! Unless, of course, she wanted them to fire her, which Millie doubted was the case.

Millie shut off the water and grabbed a clean, white towel from the metal rack above the toilet. She quickly dried off, ran a comb through her shoulder length hair and pulled it away from her face. She slipped into her work uniform and headed topside to search for Andy.

She crossed the dark auditorium and climbed the set of stairs off to the side. Red velvet curtains covered the stage. Millie grabbed the edge of the curtain, pulled it aside and stepped backstage.

Millie could hear muffled voices coming from the direction of the makeup area.

Zack, one of the dancers and one of Millie's favorite staff members, caught Millie's eye. He gave a small wave and met her halfway across the stage. "I watched Andy's Taser demonstration earlier," he said.

Millie nodded. "Yeah, I thought I was a goner."

"I did, too." Zack shot her a wicked smile. "You should've seen the look on your face!"

Millie could envision the deer-in-the-headlights look she probably had. "Oh, I can just imagine."

"Of course, your expression wasn't nearly as entertaining as Andy's reaction to being tased," he chuckled.

"Zack! We're ready!" A female voice rang out from somewhere in the dressing room.

Zack shot a glance toward the back. "I gotta run!" He dashed out of the area and Millie continued to walk towards Andy's office.

A faint beam of light shone over the top of the half partition wall that separated his office from the stage.

Andy sat hunched over, his head mere inches from an open notebook as he studied the papers in front of him.

"You should be wearing reading glasses."

Andy lifted his head, his bespectacled face staring into hers. "Huh?"

"Never mind," Millie mumbled. She pulled out a chair and plopped down. "What'cha doing?"

Andy tapped the tip of his pen on top of the notebook. "I'm going over this week's schedule. I've been mulling over a new headliner event I plan to pitch to the captain and want to get your thoughts."

Millie leaned in. The schedule they had now was a good one. It started with the Welcome Aboard show the first night. The show highlighted the talents of the dancers, the magician, the comedian, etc. Then there was the Heart and Homes Show where guests – couples – competed against each other to see which couple knew their spouse best.

The other nights consisted of a stage production show and the magician's show. The comedian rounded out the headliners.

When the current passengers got off, a new wave of passengers boarded and they started the schedule all over again...

"What are you thinking?" Millie was curious.

"Replace the Heart and Homes show with a dating game." He paused. "Do you remember that American show years ago called *The Dating Game,* the one where an eligible bachelor or bachelorette asked three people who they couldn't see behind a wall, a set of quirky questions and then that person picked one of them for a blind date?"

Millie raised a brow. It sounded intriguing. They had plenty of singles on board their ship. In fact, the *Mix and Mingle Singles Party* had one of the highest numbers of attendees week after week. Why not mix it up and quite possibly make a love connection?

Andy could see the wheels spinning in Millie's mind. He pressed on.

"We could offer them a complimentary couple's massage or a romantic dinner for two in one of the upscale restaurants." He paused. "I have an idea! What about an excursion to one of the islands or a romantic picnic for two on a secluded beach...hmm?"

The idea was growing on her. Who wouldn't love to see a little budding romance on board a cruise ship?

"I think it's worth pitching. It sounds intriguing," she said.

Andy snapped his fingers. "Hey! You could be one of the first contestants!"

Millie shook her head. "Oh no you don't! I am not the least bit interested in being the evening entertainment." Millie turned the tables. "Why don't YOU do it? It's your idea," she pointed out.

Andy grinned. "Scratch that idea."

Today was the last day for the current group of passengers and tomorrow would be turnaround day – the busiest day of the week.

Andy handed Millie her schedule for the rest of the afternoon. She slipped on her reading glasses and pulled the sheet close. It consisted of checking on the various activities around the ship, including a pie-eating contest, a wine tasting demonstration and bingo.

Sometimes Millie wanted to pinch herself. None of this seemed like work!

"Looks good." Millie folded the sheet of paper into thirds and tucked it in her front pocket.

She pushed back the chair. "It's time to get Scout."

Andy looked up from his schedule. "You hear about the food poisoning down in the officer's dining room?"

Millie nodded. "Yeah. Annette swears she tried the lobster bisque before it ever left the kitchen, so somewhere between the kitchen and the dining room, something happened."

Andy nodded. He picked up his glasses and stuck the earpiece in his mouth. "This could spell big trouble for Annette," he warned. "It's the second time in less than 24 hours that someone has fallen ill from food linked to her and the kitchen."

Millie swallowed hard. She hated the thought of her friend losing her job. "I believe Annette. If she said she didn't poison the food, then she didn't."

"I believe her, too," Andy agreed. "You do know that her contract as Director of Food and

Beverage expires in two weeks and it hasn't been renewed yet. In fact, I heard that several applications have crossed Donovan Sweeney's desk, and that some of them are other employees who meet the requirements."

Millie's brow formed a deep "V." Was someone sabotaging Annette in an attempt to get her canned so that person could swoop in and snag her job? "So it's possible someone is out to get Annette fired."

Andy nodded. "But you didn't hear me say that."

Millie wandered out of the office and across the stage. It sure sounded to her like someone was poisoning the ship's crew on purpose. Her blood chilled at a terrifying thought. *What if the saboteur planned to poison the guests next?*

Chapter 3

The bridge was Millie's next stop. She could not wait to see her pint-size pal, Scout.

She had missed him yesterday since it had been a port day. Millie had spent part of her day onshore picking up shampoo, deodorant and other items that were super-expensive on board the ship.

Her prized purchase of the day was her favorite potato chips, which she was only able to find in certain ports. Grand Cayman was one of them.

Grand Cayman was one of the safer ports that Siren of the Seas visited. It was an expensive island for both tourists and residents, and Millie couldn't imagine how much it cost to actually live there.

Today was the last sea day with the current group of passengers, and it was supposed to be a walk in the park, except now she was worried about her friend, Annette.

Millie stepped into the bridge. Captain Armati was in the center of the room, studying a large computer screen. He caught Millie's eye and smiled.

"Good morning, Millie. Well, guess it's afternoon now. " The warmth in his voice traveled to his eyes. Her heart fluttered. A warm tingle started in the top of her head and spread all the way down to her toes.

"Good morning, Captain Armati."

A few weeks ago, Captain Armati had invited Millie to dine with him in his quarters. Just the thought of that dinner caused her pulse to quicken.

He waved her down the narrow hall that led to his private apartment.

Ingrid Kozlov, the only other occupant in the bridge, glared at Millie as she passed by. Millie was growing accustomed to the woman's glares. For some reason, Ingrid did not care for Millie one bit, not that Millie had ever done anything to make her angry.

The only logical explanation Millie could come up with was that maybe Ingrid had a thing for the captain and she viewed Millie as her competition.

Captain Armati punched the buttons on the keypad above the doorknob. He waited for the click, then opened the door and held it for Millie.

A brown ball of fur raced across the floor and climbed on top of Millie's shoe. Two small paws batted at her ankle.

Millie lifted Scout and brought him close to her face. He promptly licked every part of Millie that his tiny little pink tongue could reach.

"He missed you yesterday," Captain Armati told her.

Scout wiggled until Millie set him back on the floor where he ran circles around her feet. Scout was ready to start his day!

Captain Armati tucked his arms behind his back and stared thoughtfully at Scout. "You heard about Captain Vitale."

Millie nodded. "Yes. How terrible." Millie knew this was her one chance to speak her mind.

"Annette and I are friends. I don't believe for one minute she's responsible for Captain Vitale's poisoning."

She went on to explain how Annette and Amit had tasted the lobster bisque before the dish was taken to the dining room and how they hadn't gotten ill.

She could see he was listening to what she had to say so she rushed on, telling him how Annette's contract was up and that several others – other staff – had applied for the position.

"Hmm. So you think someone is trying to oust Annette and then swoop in and take her job?"

Millie wasn't 100% certain this was the case but it was the most plausible explanation. "I have a strong hunch this is what is happening."

Captain Armati walked to the door. Millie and Scout trailed behind. "I am sympathetic to Annette's position, but I cannot risk having more of my crew, let alone passengers, fall ill, especially if it's preventable."

Millie knew that. It meant she had a short amount of time to get to the bottom of the mystery and she was going to start right now – with Annette.

Millie and Scout made their way across the ship and down to Deck 1 and the crew quarters. Millie set Scout on the floor and watched as he darted back and forth across the I-95 corridor.

Scout got miles of smiles and a few of the crew even stopped to pet him. Scout ate it up.

They stopped in front of Annette's cabin. Millie tapped lightly on the door.

"Go away!"

Determined that Annette had had enough time to wallow in her self-pity, she knocked again, this time harder.

"I said – go away!"

Millie pressed her face in the crack of the door. "I am not going anywhere, not until you let me in," she threatened.

The door flew open. Millie started to tumble forward, which would have been hilarious if not for the look on her friend's face. Millie could see that Annette had been crying. Her eyes were red and puffy.

Millie closed the door behind Scout and her and settled onto the edge of the bed. Annette pulled out the desk chair and slumped down.

Millie could see it was going to take a little tough love to get through to Annette. "Annette

Delacroix, I didn't peg you as a quitter," she challenged.

Annette shrugged. "Maybe you don't know me, after all."

Millie set Scout on the floor. He promptly darted over to Annette and licked her bare ankle. She frowned and glanced down. "Crazy dog," she muttered.

Scout let out a low whine and slunk back to Millie, who picked him up and set him on her lap. "You aren't used to rejection, huh fella?" She scratched his chin.

"I know your contract is almost up and there are others gunning for your job," Millie told her.

Annette didn't answer. She stuck her chin on top of her fist and closed her eyes.

Millie brought out the big guns. "We need to get to the bottom of this and figure out who is throwing you under the bus! Someone, somewhere on the ship is intentionally making people ill. Unsuspecting passengers could be next!"

"That would be horrible," Annette mumbled.

Millie snapped her fingers. "Exactly. Neither of us wants to see one more crew – or a single passenger - poisoned so we need to start working on this case. Pronto!"

Annette lifted her gaze. Her eyes met Millie's eyes. "But...how? How do we figure out who is behind this?"

"We need to get our hands on the list of crewmembers who applied for your job." Now all Millie had to do was figure out where the applications were.

Millie had another thought. They could solve the mystery quickly if they knew who delivered the dish to the officer's dining room. "Who took the dish downstairs to the dining room?"

Annette's brow furrowed, she tapped the side of her cheek with her index finger. "Well...I handed it to Amit but he said he didn't deliver the tray."

"If he didn't, who did?"

Annette brightened as she realized they might be onto something. She jumped from her chair. "I have no idea, but it's time to find out."

Millie was relieved to see Annette had bounced back. She followed Annette out of the room and up to the galley.

Amit was nowhere in sight. It was as if he had vanished into thin air.

Annette headed to the veggie prep area and approached one of the crew who was hard at work slicing tomatoes. "Where is Amit?"

The worker looked around. "I don't know. I haven't seen him in a while now. He was frosting sugar cookies last I saw."

Annette and Millie headed to the other side of the galley, to the dessert prep area. The place was a bustle of activity – and it smelled heavenly.

Even Scout noticed. His small black nose poked out of his carrier as he sniffed the air.

Annette approached one of the workers, bent over a side table. "Raj, have you seen Amit?"

Raj shook his head and continued piping frosting on top of a row of cupcakes. Millie's mouth watered. They looked delicious. Chocolate cupcakes with some kind of cream cheese frosting if she had to guess...

"No, Miss Annette. He told me a while ago that he'd be right back but I not see him come back," he explained in his heavy accent.

Annette shoved her hand on her hip. Amit should have been in the kitchen working. She glanced up at the clock. It was well past noon now and his lunch break wasn't until two. She wondered where on earth he could have gone.

Millie leaned in. "Maybe he got sick after all," she whispered in Annette's ear.

Annette frowned. "Let's check his cabin."

The girls strolled out of the galley, down the long corridor and back to the crew quarters. Amit's room was on the opposite end of the ship, near the back, or in nautical terms, aft.

Annette stopped abruptly in front of a cabin door and tapped lightly. They waited. She tried again, this time louder but there was still no answer. The third time, she balled her hands into fists and pounded.

"I don't think he's in there," Millie said.

Annette's shoulders sagged. "I'm not sure if that's a good sign or a bad sign."

"Let's take a peek in the crew mess hall and lounge," Millie suggested.

The girls trudged back down the long corridor and headed to the crew mess hall first. They stood near the entrance and surveyed the crowd. The room was packed. Millie carefully studied the occupants. Amit wasn't one of them.

Next, they headed to the lounge, which was deader than a doornail. There was no one inside, which wasn't a surprise. It was only late at night and into the wee hours of the morning that the lounge came to life.

Millie had no firsthand experience, but she heard the rumors of the wild parties that went on at all hours of the night.

Annette closed the door behind them. "I guess I'll just wait for him to reappear in the kitchen."

They made their way past the crew mess, which was on the left. The crew mess was directly across from the officer's dining room.

Millie had a sudden urge to stop and peek inside. She reached for the handle. "I'll take a quick look in here."

She turned the knob, slowly pushed the door open and stuck her head around the corner.

There, standing off to one side, talking to another crewmember that Millie didn't recognize, was Amit.

He caught a glimpse of Millie and waved.

Annette deftly sidestepped Millie and entered the room. "Shouldn't you be working?"

Amit had the decency to look embarrassed. He gave a small bow. "Yes, Miss Annette."

Without uttering a single word, the other man slunk past the girls and out the door.

Annette jerked a thumb to where the stranger had just exited. "What was that all about?"

"I was asking Suri if he delivered the lobster bisque to the dining room," Amit admitted.

Millie was relieved. That meant that Amit cared about Annette's innocence and it appeared that he was trying to help.

Annette leaned in. "Did he?" she asked.

Amit shook his head. "No. Suri said he left it in the warmer bay for a brief moment and when he returned, the dish had disappeared."

Amit shoved his hands in his front pockets. "I'm sorry, Miss Annette. I'm trying to help."

Annette patted Amit's arm. "I appreciate that, Amit. We need to figure out who delivered the dish to the dining room."

Millie frowned. Maybe they could hit it from another angle. Try to figure out who was in the dining room at the time. There had to be someone who could identify the person or persons that delivered the dish.

Things were getting a bit mucky. Annette prepared the dish. She and Amit both tasted the dish. She gave it to Amit to deliver. Amit, in turn, handed it to Suri, who left the dish unattended in the warming bay – which meant someone may have had an opportunity to tinker with the dish before it was even taken down to the officer's dining room!

The girls trudged back to the kitchen. Millie stopped outside the kitchen entrance. It was time for Scout and Millie to start their rounds. "Let's meet later tonight. Maybe by then we'll have more clues."

Millie decided not to tell Annette that she planned to try to get her hands on those applications – somehow. This case wasn't going to be as cut and dried as Millie first thought!

Chapter 4

Scout and Millie wandered onto the lido deck first. The two of them made it just in time to watch the pie-eating contest.

Lined up against one wall was a long row of tables, filled with whipped cream pies, as far as the eye could see.

Standing behind the tables with their hands tied behind their backs was a single row of roughly a dozen passengers. Off to one end and holding a stopwatch was one of the singers. Millie couldn't remember his name. He was a good-looking young man with sandy blonde hair and a mischievous smile. He caught Millie's eye and grinned.

Millie set Scout on the deck and they wandered front and center to watch the competition.

"On your mark! Get set! GO!"

The contestants buried their faces into the first pie as they rushed to finish one before moving on to the next. Three pies in, one of the junior passengers - a young man with a sharp crew cut and face coated with a thick layer of whipped cream - was the first to drop out.

The crowd showered him with a round of applause as Millie untied his hands and handed him a towel from a nearby stack. "Good job!"

The rest of the contestants plowed through several more pies until one by one, they dropped out of the contest.

It was down to two remaining contestants. One was a man that reminded Millie of Brody, the bouncer, and the other a young woman that couldn't have weighed more than 90 pounds soaking wet. They were neck and neck, or in this case pie and pie, in a dead heat.

Neither contestant seemed even remotely close to defeat. Millie glanced down the length of the table. They were running out of pies!

The host of the contest strolled over to Millie and stood silently by her side. She glanced down at his tag: *Kevin*.

Kevin lifted a whistle to his lips and blew. "Tie!" he yelled to the contestants as the crowd erupted in applause.

Both lifted pie-covered faces and grinned through a thick haze of whipped cream. The roving camera crew snapped several shots of the champions as Millie loosened the ropes that secured their hands. The two of them joined hands and raised them together in triumph!

Millie grabbed a nearby microphone and approached the couple. "That was an exciting contest. How do you feel?"

The man rubbed his stomach. "Hungry. When does the buffet open?" he joked.

The woman lifted an index finger, wiped a glob of creaminess from around her eyes and popped it into her mouth. "Good to the last bite."

Kevin stepped forward. He held a small, plastic trophy out to each of them. "Way to go!"

Millie held out her hand. "Congratulations...err?"

The woman spoke up. "Kelly." She pointed to the man standing next to her. "This is my husband, Mike."

Millie gazed from one to the other. "You two are married?"

Mike squeezed Kelly's hand. "Yes, ma'am, we are."

Millie snorted. "You two must have a heck of a grocery bill."

After the crowd dispersed, Millie helped Kevin clear the mess, along with other members of the kitchen staff.

"Thanks for the help, Millie." He glanced down at Scout, who sat off near the edge of the action and watched. "And your little furry friend."

The crew loaded the tables onto a cart and rolled them away.

Millie lifted Scout, afraid that someone might not see him and roll the cart over the top of him.

Kevin dropped to his knees and leaned forward. His hand got as far as hovering over Scout's head when Scout's ears flattened and he let out a low warning growl.

Kevin jerked his hand back. "I guess he doesn't like me."

Millie had never seen Scout act like that. He loved everyone who stopped by to pet him or talk to him. "I'm sorry, Kevin. I don't know what has gotten into Scout. Maybe it's the heat."

Kevin nodded. "No problem." He shrugged. "I'll see you around. Thanks again."

Kevin rose to his feet, turned on his heel, and strolled across the deck, whistling a catchy tune until he disappeared from sight.

Millie lifted Scout eye level. "What's up with that, mister? He was only trying to pet you," she scolded.

Scout opened his mouth and his little pink tongue dropped out. Maybe he was hangry – hungry and angry, and it was making him cranky.

Millie slipped Scout into his carrier and adjusted the strap on her shoulder before they headed into Waves, the buffet area.

She grabbed a tray from the end of the line. Today's themed menu included foods from the featured island, Grand Cayman.

Millie selected several tempting dishes that she thought both she and Scout would enjoy – not that she gave Scout more than just a taste since he had such a tiny tummy.

She grabbed a set of tongs and scooped a piece of fish onto her plate. She also scooped a few conch fritters, a large spoonful of rice and a slice of beef – for Scout. She didn't dare give him anything too spicy – just in case.

Millie balanced her tray, stopping at the beverage station for a tall glass of ice water before they headed outside and up one flight of stairs.

She had recently stumbled upon a small eating area that was perfect. It was close to the mini golf course and away from the crowds. She chose this spot – just in case Scout needed to take a plastic palm tree break.

Millie climbed to the top of the stairs and started around the side when she caught a glimpse of Frank Bauer, the head of maintenance. It looked as if he was working on something off in the corner.

The sun was high in the sky but there was still a bit of shade as Millie and Scout settled in at the small bistro table. She unzipped the bag and waited while Scout wandered out of the carrier and onto the rattan armchair.

Next, Millie pulled Scout's water dish from a pocket in the side of the carrier and filled it with cold water. She set it on the chair, right next to Scout, who promptly drank the water.

Millie sliced off tiny slivers of beef and set them on a paper napkin. She set the napkin on the other side of the water dish.

Scout licked her hand and began to nibble on his goodies.

Millie placed her napkin in her lap and bowed her head to pray over her food.

The two of them watched the guests stroll by as they enjoyed their lunch. Several of the passengers stopped to talk to Scout and pat his head. Not once did he growl at any of them. She wondered what it was about Kevin that Scout didn't like – or sensed.

After they finished eating, Millie stacked the dirty dishes on top of the tray and carried it to the trash container. She dumped the trash inside and stacked the dishes in the dirty dish bin.

She hooked Scout's bright blue leash to his collar, then slung his bag over her shoulder. They walked all the way around the mini golf course and over to Frank Bauer, who was still off to the side.

Captain Armati was there, too. They were peering behind a set of white plastic partition walls.

Although Millie often saw Captain Armati wandering around the ship, he typically stuck close to where passengers congregated.

Scout strained to pull Millie along when he spotted the captain. "*Yip!*"

Frank and Captain Armati swung around when they heard Scout's greeting. "Hello Millie."

Scout promptly hopped on Armati's shiny black shoe. The captain lifted his beloved dog and Scout licked his chin.

Frank reached out to pat the top of Scout's head.

Millie frowned. Frank was a complete stranger to Scout, yet Scout didn't seem to mind in the least when he got close.

Captain set Scout on the ground and turned to Millie. "You're just in time. You must have read my mind."

Millie raised a brow. "Oh really? Why?"

He clasped his hands together. "We have a surprise for you," he answered.

He waved Millie through the wide opening in the plastic panels.

Millie peeked around the white wall and gasped when she caught sight of the interior.

To the right was a padded lounge chair and small blue table.

To the left was what Millie could only describe as a mini, miniature golf course – Scout-size. The green space was dotted with small, plastic palm trees, surrounded by sand traps. Smack dab in the center of the green was a sunken swimming pool!

The three of them and Scout stepped inside the enclosed space.

Millie unhooked Scout's leash and he darted over to his oasis where he promptly watered the nearest palm tree, then pawed at a section of sand.

After that, he patrolled the perimeter, starting at the edge of the green. He made his way to the other end where he squeezed in between the wall and the padded deck chair before he turned around and headed back.

Millie watched as Scout sprinted across the fake grass and made a beeline for the pool. Scout jumped into the swimming pool and frolicked in the water. Millie could almost see the smile on his face.

"He loves it!" She turned and smiled brightly at the captain. "You did this for Scout?"

Captain Armati nodded his head, pleased that he could make Scout – and Millie happy. "It's for both of you."

"We have been working on this project for several days now," Frank told her.

Captain slapped a hand on Frank's shoulder. "I couldn't have done it alone. Thanks to Frank's creativity since we have limited building supplies on board."

Frank's face beamed. He stepped over to the opening in the door. Millie hadn't noticed in all the excitement, but there was a plastic gate attached to one of the partitions.

Frank unlatched a hook and pulled the small gray gate across the opening. It was a custom-made doggie gate! "You can close this so that Scout doesn't sneak out when you're not looking," he explained.

Millie bent down and tested the gate as she pulled it back and forth across the opening.

Captain Armati pointed to the pool and Scout, who was having a grand old time, splashing around. "There's a plug in the bottom. You can drain the water when you're done using it."

On the wall, next to the green, was a small hand faucet. He pointed to the faucet. "The next time you want to use it, all you have to do is fill it back up with clean tap water."

Millie shook her head in amazement. They had thought of everything! At least she thought they had until Frank stepped behind the lounge chair and bent down to open a small box attached to the floor. "We even brought a few balls out so you can play catch."

Millie set Scout's carrier next to the lounge chair. She wasn't sure who was more excited. It had to be Scout, who hopped out of the pool and began batting one of the balls across the floor.

"Thank you so much. You have no idea what this means to me." She pointed at Scout. "To us."

"Of course, other passengers may take advantage of it," the captain warned.

Millie didn't mind. It wasn't really hers anyway, and she was more than willing to share!

The captain and Frank left Scout and Millie inside their little oasis as they headed back down the steps.

Millie plopped into the lounge chair and reached for one of the small balls. Scout was into the game as he chased the ball across the enclosed area and brought it back to her.

They played catch for a few more minutes before Scout decided it was time for another swim. The mini pool was just big enough for him to pick up enough steam to paddle his little legs back and forth.

They stayed in their special oasis for as long as Millie dared before it was time to report to the wine tasting on Deck 6.

"C'mon, Scout!" Scout reluctantly hopped out of the pool and wandered over to Millie. He was soaking wet from the top of his head to the tip of his toenails. Scout did a doggie shake and a small spray of water droplets pelted Millie's ankle.

It would have been nice to have something to dry him. The thought had no more popped into her head when she noticed a small, metal rack hanging on the wall. Inside the rack was a tidy stack of hand towels – perfect for Scout.

Millie grinned and shook her head. Captain Armati and Frank had thought of everything!

Millie dried Scout as best she could – or as best as he would let her - before she snapped the leash on his collar and slid the special gate to the side so they could exit. She cast one last glance back at their new hangout. Captain Armati was full of surprises!

Chapter 5

Andy was in charge of the wine tasting class. Scout and Millie arrived just in time to catch the start. Millie had never attended one before and she assumed the reason Andy had asked her to make an appearance was that at some point in time, he was going to put her in charge!

Millie collected the tickets from attendees while Andy arranged various vintage wine bottles on top of the u-shaped table.

The sommelier, Pierre LeBlanc, took center stage as he hooked a small microphone to his lapel and started to explain the different wines to the passengers. He also made suggestions on what foods to pair the wine.

Millie and Andy stood on either side of Pierre and poured small samples of wine in guests' glasses as he made his way along the table.

Millie caught Andy red-handed tasting Bordeaux, a red wine. His gaze met hers and he winked. Millie grinned. He lifted the glass as if to say, "You should try it," but Millie shook her head.

What other job allowed you to drink on the job, unless, of course, you were a sommelier!

After the wine tasting ended, Millie helped Pierre and Andy clear the area.

Millie headed up to Ocean Treasures to check in with Cat.

Passengers squeezed into every single square inch of space in front of the shop. The final day of the cruise featured 50% off sales, which enticed guests to make a few impulse purchases.

It was Cat's least favorite day of the cruise. The place was a zoo!

Millie wove her way through the thick crowd as she headed to the back of the store and the cash register where Cat was ringing up a steady stream of customers.

She looked a bit frazzled and her perfectly coiffed beehive hairdo was a bit off kilter – a sure sign that Cat was stressing out.

She caught Millie's eye and held up a finger, motioning her off to the side. Millie waited until there was a lull in the crowd before Scout and she stepped to the register.

"You need to stop by the kitchen to see Annette. She has a plan," Cat muttered from the corner of her mouth.

Millie nodded. "What..." She started to ask what plan, but by then there was another group of passengers waiting to check out. Cat plastered a smile on her face and picked up the customer's purchases.

Millie squeezed back through the chaotic scene. Her claustrophobia kicked into high gear and her heart began to race.

Safely outside and away from the chaos, Millie breathed a sigh of relief. She set Scout on the floor and the two of them headed to the stairwell.

Millie avoided elevators like the plague, having had a traumatic experience not long ago when one of the glass elevators in the atrium had malfunctioned and trapped her inside, in between floors.

Scout didn't seem to mind the stairs and he kept pace with Millie as they made their way down to the deck where the kitchen was located.

They wandered to the back entrance and slipped in through the swinging side door. The door got little use since most of the kitchen staff – and wait staff – used the revolving doors that separated the galley from the main dining rooms.

Millie could hear Annette before she could see her. "We must make 100% certain that the food that leaves this kitchen is safe. We don't need a single passenger falling ill or..."

Millie peeked around the corner. Annette paced back and forth in front of the kitchen staff. She reminded Millie of a drill sergeant.

"...or else," she made a slicing motion across her neck, "...off with our heads!"

She stopped in her tracks. "Got it?"

The group nodded.

Annette thumped her fist on the stainless steel prep table. "Now back to work," she roared.

Millie came up behind her. "That was quite a pep talk!"

Annette whirled around. "Like that? I'm just rallying the troops." She winked.

Annette grabbed Millie's arm and dragged her toward the walk-in freezer. "I have an idea on how we can get our hands on those applications," she whispered.

"How?"

Annette answered the question with one of her own. "You have a master key card that unlocks almost every door on board the ship, right?"

Millie nodded. "Yeah." She wasn't sure she liked where this was going...

"Well, I found out that all of the applications are in Donovan Sweeney's office," Annette said.

Donovan Sweeney was the ship's purser. Donovan was like the bank. He controlled all the money, all the expenses, all the crew tips and pay and apparently, all the new hires!

"How did you find that out?" Millie asked.

Annette shook her head. "It doesn't matter. What matters is that we get our hands on those applications!"

"So your plan..."

Annette cut Millie off. "We sneak into Donovan's office and snap a few quick pictures of the applications – but only the ones that applied for my job. Voila! We have our list of suspects!"

Visions of Dave Patterson, the ship's head of security, throwing her – throwing them all – in the slammer, filled Millie's head. She had done some dumb things in her life but never had she intentionally done something that could put her in jail.

"You do know that Donovan's office also houses the ship's safe where all the money is kept?" Millie pointed out.

Annette lifted her fingernail and picked at the edge. "True...but I don't plan on getting caught."

"What does Cat think?" Millie asked.

Cat had already experienced the inside of the ship's jail because of Annette and Millie. Well, it wasn't directly their fault. That particular incident had been a huge misunderstanding...

Annette waved a dismissive hand. "Oh! She doesn't know yet but I'm sure she'll be fine with it!"

Millie wasn't convinced. The three of them were going to sneak into Donovan's office, rummage around in his desk and take pictures. She had a sudden thought.

"What if there's a camera inside his office?"

"There is." Annette nodded. "I've already got that covered! I know exactly where the applications are being kept and I know the exact position of the camera."

She grabbed a crisp, white tablecloth from a shelf under the counter and with the flick of her wrist, opened it. "The camera is right inside the door. I slip in the room first, toss the tablecloth on top of the camera and then when we're done, I take it off on my way out."

One thing was certain: Annette had given the scheme some thought, but there were still unanswered questions.

"Won't security notice the blank camera screen and decide to investigate?"

"True." Annette admitted. "That's why we have to be in and out of there fast. I timed it. We will have approximately 15 seconds before security arrives. That's why all three of us need to go in. Divide and conquer."

Millie thrust her hand on her hip. "Why don't you just ask Donovan for a list of the applicants instead of going through all this?"

Annette's shoulders sagged. "I already did and he said that it's against company policy...something about employee privacy or some such nonsense."

Millie still wasn't convinced. She could see the whole thing going horribly wrong. "Let me think about it."

Scout and she headed for the back door. "We'll rendezvous here at 1:45 a.m. sharp," Annette called after her. "That's when security is busy closing down the bars and it gives us the best chance of a successful operation."

Millie grabbed the door handle. "I guess," she caved.

She pushed the door open and let Scout go ahead of her.

Millie rolled her eyes and groaned. "What have I gotten myself into?"

Scout, completely unconcerned with Millie's dilemma, trotted off down the corridor. It was time for bingo.

Millie's friend, Zack, was working the bingo sessions and she was excited that they would be working together, something they were rarely able to do.

She lifted her furry sidekick, wandered into the theater and up the stage steps. She clipped Scout's leash to his collar and then wrapped the leash around the leg of the bingo table.

Today Millie would be in charge of selling bingo cards. Business was brisk. The line was long and it took longer than normal since almost all of the passengers that purchased bingo cards also stopped to say "hi" to Scout.

Zack bent down to pat Scout's head. He gave Millie a quick hug. "Hey, Millie. I haven't seen you hanging out behind the stage lately."

Millie nodded. "Andy is keeping me busy."

"I suppose you already heard about Captain Vitale getting food poisoning? That's the second person in less than a day."

Millie thumbed through the stack of bingo cards. "Yeah. Annette is taking this hard. The food is coming from her kitchen."

Zack bent down and lowered his voice. "Don't tell Annette, but someone started a petition, calling for Annette's resignation."

Millie's heart plummeted. "Who would do such a horrible thing?"

"Someone gunning for her job since her contract is up," he answered. "They have over 50 signatures. I refused to sign."

This was much worse than Millie had imagined. If the petition got enough signatures, Captain Armati wouldn't have much of a choice but to let Annette go. After all, if the crew wouldn't eat her food, why should the passengers?

Millie didn't see much choice but to go along with Annette's plan to sneak into Donovan's office and try to find out who might be behind all of this!

Zack turned to go.

"Wait!" Millie stopped him. "Do you have any idea who might want Annette's job?"

Zack shrugged his shoulders. "The only name I heard being tossed around is Annette's right hand man, Amit."

Chapter 6

Millie's mouth fell open. *Amit had applied for Annette's job?* She remembered the time Annette had chewed Amit out when he substituted margarine for the lobster dish. Did he hold a grudge?

Although Annette could be a little rough around the edges at times, she had a heart of gold and she was loyal to a fault.

Amit seemed like a nice enough fellow and Millie never would have imagined him capable of stabbing Annette in the back like that. Of course, one never knew for sure...

Annette had told Millie that she put Amit in charge of delivering the bisque to the officer's dining room. Amit said he turned it over to Suri, who admitted he left the dish in the warming bay.

Could it be that Amit doubled-back, poisoned the bisque and then planned on Suri taking the blame?

She would just have to wait until tonight to find out if Amit had indeed submitted an application for Annette's job – that is, if they weren't caught in the act!

Millie had no time to dwell on Amit's possible double-crossing.

Bingo was a lively session and there were several winners. Today, the final day of the cruise, Siren of the Seas gave away the grand prize: a free, seven-day cruise for two. Millie was excited to see a young couple; newlyweds if she remembered correctly, win the grand prize.

Millie wandered around the theater and picked up the used bingo cards that littered the floor and chairs, left behind by passengers.

When she finished cleaning up, she decided to make a quick stop by the bridge to thank Captain

Armati for the little retreat that she and Scout would enjoy for a long time to come.

Her heart sunk when she stepped into the bridge. Captain Vitale was noticeably absent.

Captain Armati turned and smiled as the two of them stepped into the bridge. "Did you have a chance to enjoy your new hangout?"

Millie nodded and grinned. "Scout didn't want to get out of the pool."

"Woof!" He agreed.

Millie set him on the floor and he scampered over to say hello to Ingrid Kozlov who was off in the corner, studying a computer screen.

For the first time that Millie could remember, the woman actually smiled as she pet Scout and watched as he danced around her feet.

Millie turned to face the captain. "How is Captain Vitale feeling?"

Armati frowned. "He is too ill to work today. We need to find out what is going on in that kitchen."

Millie lifted her hand in a mock salute. "I'm on it," she assured him.

Perhaps that wasn't the best answer. Millie had a penchant for sticking her nose in where it didn't belong.

Captain lifted a brow. "Try to stay out of trouble." He stressed the word *try*.

Millie turned to go and then paused. "Captain Vitale, does he blame Annette?"

Technically, Donovan Sweeney was in charge of the kitchen and kitchen staff while Captain Vitale was in charge of the rest of the crew, but that didn't mean that Vitale couldn't go over Donovan's head and have her fired. Captain Vitale was second in command while Donovan Sweeney was right below him as third in command.

Captain Armati shook his head. "No. Captain Vitale is a fair man. He would need to see proof that Annette intentionally poisoned crew or passengers before he would make such a decision."

Millie's shoulders sagged in relief. The relief was short-lived.

"Of course, that doesn't mean he couldn't decide that someone would be a better fit for the next contract."

That was Millie's fear. Annette's employment teetered on finding out who was trying to get rid of her!

Scout and Millie wandered out of the bridge. There was no way she could turn Annette down and not try to find out who had applied for her job.

The rest of the evening dragged by as Millie's mind drifted to the coming hours. She made a quick stop to see Cat before heading up to the lido deck to check on the deck party.

"Did Annette tell you about the plan?" Cat asked before Millie had a chance to mention it.

She nodded. "What do you think?"

Cat rolled her eyes. "That I don't want to end up in jail again," she moaned. "Seems like every time the two of you drag me into your misadventures, I always end up in hot water."

"You?" Millie gasped. "What about me? I mean, I'm the one that has the key that unlocks the door!"

"True," Cat admitted. "But what choice do we have? Stand by and watch them fire Annette?"

Millie almost told Cat what Zack had said about Amit applying for Annette's job but something stopped her. She trusted Cat but she wasn't sure if she trusted her not to spill the beans to Annette. On top of that, Millie wasn't 100% certain it was true.

Right now, that information was just a rumor. If he had applied, they would find out soon enough.

By the time Millie dropped Scout off, she was on pins and needles and her conscience was pricking her.

Captain Armati met her at the door. He held it wide. "Please. Come in, Millie."

Millie stepped through the apartment door and set Scout on the floor. He trotted over to the captain who picked him up and tucked him in the crook of his arm.

"Are you off duty?"

Millie nodded.

"Care for a glass of wine?"

Millie's eyes wandered to the chilled wine on the table. It reminded her of the night, not long ago, he had invited her to dinner. It had been a romantic evening.

Since then, although the captain had been warm and friendly, he hadn't asked again. Millie was beginning to wonder if she had said something wrong.

Millie nodded. "That would be lovely."

Maybe a glass of wine would calm her nerves seeing how she was only hours away from breaking a company policy.

The captain poured wine into two glasses and the three of them stepped out onto the balcony.

Scout made a beeline for his grassy area before heading back inside to grab a stuffed monkey twice his size. He clamped his jaw on the monkey's tail and dragged it out onto the deck. They watched as he struggled to tug it over the threshold.

"Sometimes he crawls inside his toy box and falls asleep and I can't find him because he blends in."

Millie burst out laughing. The vision of Scout sprawled out on top of his toys cracked her up. "I'd love to see that sometime."

Captain nodded. "Perhaps you will."

Millie blushed. She lifted her wine glass to hide her flaming cheeks.

Captain Armati changed the subject. "Andy proposed a new show to me earlier today during our weekly meeting. It was something about a dating game."

Millie had almost forgotten about it. So much had happened since morning, starting out with the Taser demonstration, then leaping right into the food poisoning.

"I like the idea." Millie twirled the wine around in her glass before she lifted it to her lips to take another sip. It was going down smooth...too smooth.

Armati nodded. "Me, too. Cruise ships can be the perfect spot for a budding romance. I have several friends that met and married on board a ship."

Millie nearly choked on the wine as she sucked in a breath and tried to swallow at the same time. *Cough!*

Captain Armati patted her back. "Are you okay?"

Millie's eyes watered. "Went down the wrong way," she sputtered. She coughed a couple more times and pounded her chest. "Much better."

She moved the subject to a safer topic. "Speaking of ships, how much longer are you on before your break?" She had heard that the captain's contract only lasted about six months.

Armati lowered his glass and gazed out at the vast ocean. "Next month. I have a six week break."

He smiled at Millie. "But I already signed on for another six months so I'll be back."

Millie frowned. She hoped that she hadn't sounded like she was fishing. On second thought, maybe she was. She stared down at her half-empty wine glass. *Loose lips sink ships.*

They finished their wine and Millie followed the captain back inside. She set her glass on the table and turned to go. "Thank you for the wine."

"Perhaps we could have dinner again sometime?" he asked.

Millie felt beads of perspiration instantly sprout up on her brow. "I-I would lo – like that!" she corrected herself.

"Good." He nodded and walked her to the door. "Scout and I shall see you tomorrow, after the new guests have boarded?"

"Of course," Millie answered. *Unless I'm in jail by then*, she added silently.

Chapter 7

Millie fiddled with the lanyard around her neck as she touched her keycard – the one with her name on it. The one that would give the girls access to Donovan's office...the lanyard that could get her fired.

On the one hand, she wanted desperately to help her friend, Annette. On the other hand, she really wanted to keep her job, but how could she tell her "no?" After all, Millie literally held the key to possibly figuring out who was poisoning the food.

The only shot they had was to get in and get out fast - and to make sure they weren't caught on camera. She gave the mission a 50/50 chance of success. She hoped the right "50" was in their favor.

Millie made her way down to the crew mess for what might be her final meal of freedom where she ran into her roommate, Sarah, and Sarah's friend, Nikki.

Nikki worked in guest services. Donovan was her immediate supervisor. Nikki seemed to like working for Donovan and she had commented several times that he was easygoing and not too strict about company policy.

Millie spied the girls as soon as she walked through the double doors. Nikki gave a small wave and Sarah motioned her over.

Millie grabbed a tray, placed it on the metal runners in front of the food display and made her way down the line. Not one single dish looked appealing as she stared at the offerings. It didn't even smell good. She knew she should eat but just the thought of it made her stomach churn.

Her heart felt heavy, as if she was waiting for a death sentence. In a way it was. She wondered what exactly would happen to them if they were caught. Would they end up in the clink? It had happened to Cat.

Would Captain Armati and Donovan kick them off the ship in the next port? The next port was Miami, so at least Millie would be close to home and not in some foreign country, left to fend for herself and figure a way home.

Last, but not least, she knew that Captain Armati and Andy would be deeply disappointed in her. They trusted her. She felt as if she would be betraying their trust. It was a no-win situation.

Millie grabbed the first thing she saw, a hot dog, along with a side salad and carried the tray to the table. She plastered a smile on her face as she set the tray in front of the empty chair.

Sarah smiled back. "Haven't seen you around at all today."

Millie plopped down in the chair. She unwrapped the silverware, set it on the table and laid the napkin in her lap. "Yeah, Andy is keeping me busy. Between Andy and Scout, my day has been hectic."

Sarah eyed her thoughtfully. "I heard your friend, Annette, is having some issues in the kitchen."

Nikki plucked a French fry from her plate, dipped it in the mound of catsup and popped it in her mouth. "She came down to guest services earlier. She went inside Donovan's office and closed the door. When they came out, Annette's face was all red, like she had been crying."

Millie's heart plummeted. Her eyes dropped to her lap. "She's a bit...distraught. She thinks someone is out to get her job."

Sarah nodded. She leaned forward. "I heard that Veronica Chang is gunning for it, which wouldn't surprise me."

Millie wrinkled her nose. *Veronica Chang?*

Veronica had started her contract the same week as Millie. She worked as first cook, and oversaw the second cook and third cook. At least that was what Annette had explained when Millie first met Veronica.

The woman was... a braggart, for lack of a better word. Everything that came out of her mouth was that she did this and she did that and one time she had served the Vice President of Majestic Cruise Lines.

When Millie dug a little deeper, Veronica finally admitted that she had plated his food but hadn't actually served him. After that, Millie took every word that came out of Veronica's mouth with a grain of salt.

Nikki nodded. "She's been hanging out in Donovan's office for days now."

"I wonder what Donovan thinks of that?" Millie asked.

"He's eating it up," Nikki said.

Millie wasn't surprised. Veronica was an attractive woman; some would say stunning. Her hair was long and silky black, her skin a smooth, olive-color and her eyes reminded Millie of a tiger. One that was about to devour its prey. They were a mesmerizing shade of amber.

Rumor had it that she had been a Miss Universe finalist a few years back. What she was doing working in the kitchen, as a first cook was a mystery to Millie.

Sarah lifted the top of her hamburger bun and removed a wilted piece of lettuce. "What about Noel?"

"Noel" was Noel Kalani. She was another beauty, similar in looks to Veronica but personality-wise, the two couldn't be more different. She was from the Hawaiian Islands and the sweetest little thing.

Noel was like a little angel, always helping Annette out in the kitchen, running here and there at Annette's beck and call with nary a complaint.

Millie was convinced Amit was madly in love with Noel. He followed her around like a puppy. She wasn't 100% certain, but it seemed that Noel liked him, too.

Amit wasn't the only one who fawned over Noel. Raj, one of the bakery staff, followed Noel around, too. Annette wondered if one day the two men would come to blows over Noel.

Millie immediately dismissed Noel as a suspect. No way would such a sweet, demure young lady be able to hatch such a diabolical plot to harm people and ruin Annette's life.

They would just have to wait until tonight to see who had actually applied for Annette's job.

After dinner, Millie headed to her cabin. Sarah and Nikki returned to work.

Millie slipped her key card in the door, waited for the *ping*, then pushed it open. She glanced down at her watch. It was only 10:30. She still had another three hours to wait.

She slipped off her shoes and crawled into her bunk, hoping to get a couple hours shuteye before the rendezvous.

She closed her eyes and started to nod off when someone began to pound on her cabin door. "Millie! Are you in there?"

Millie's eyes flew open. It sounded like Cat.

Millie scrambled out of bed, rushed over to the door and flung it open.

It was Cat. "They just airlifted Captain Vitale off the ship. He's in really bad shape!"

Chapter 8

Millie's hand flew to her lips. "Are you sure?"

Cat nodded. "Several passengers came into the store to tell me that someone was being airlifted off the ship so I quick closed the shop and ran up to the helipad. Sure enough, Captain Vitale was strapped to a gurney. They loaded him into the helicopter then took off."

Millie shoved her feet in her shoes and followed Cat out the door. They made it to the helipad in record time. A large crowd milled about.

Millie studied the crowd. "You're certain it was Captain Vitale?" Maybe she was mistaken. After all, terminally ill passengers cruised on Siren of the Seas every week. The passenger and family would plan one last hurrah, which included children, grandchildren and extended family. Often, the stress of the trip would be too much and it wasn't unusual for someone to expire while onboard. The morgue was a popular place.

Millie closed her eyes and said a quick prayer that that was the case. That it wasn't Captain Vitale.

"I got close enough to see his face. Poor Annette," Cat clucked.

Millie's eyes flew open. "Does Annette know?"

Cat nodded. "She was here before me."

The crowd began to disperse and Cat and Millie slowly made their way across the deck and down the side stairs. She wondered if Patterson had tested the bisque yet.

It was quite possible the ship did not have the necessary equipment to do that. She wished she knew what was in it. All they had to go on were hunches.

Now that Vitale had taken a turn for the worse, would the captain just up and fire Annette without a thorough investigation? He didn't strike Millie as a person given to impulse, but then she didn't know him that well.

"We better go find Annette," Millie told Cat.

Her fear was that Annette would sink into the funk again and Millie wouldn't be able to pull her out. She needn't have worried.

When the girls reached the kitchen, Annette was in the midst of a major culinary creation. Baking supplies covered the entire counter.

A thin layer of flour covered everything, including the floor. Millie also spotted eggs, milk, butter, salt, about a dozen different spices, along with several large blocks of white cheese.

They watched as Annette darted back and forth from two large kettles that were boiling on top of the stove and an enormous wooden butcher block on the edge of the stainless steel counter.

Annette grabbed a long, sharp knife and one of the blocks of cheese. She lifted the knife above her head and brought it down in one sharp motion. *Whack!* Annette cut the cheese into smaller blocks before dropping the pieces into an industrial-size shredder.

She worked like a kitchen ninja, moving so fast, Millie was afraid she was going to slice off her hand.

She acknowledged Cat and Millie's presence with a brief nod.

Cat, the braver of the two, inched her way over to the crowded counter and placed an elbow on top. "Whatcha making?"

"Just whipping up a couple pans of ravioli and fontina sauce for tomorrow night's menu." She glanced at her watch. "I mean tonight's dinner menu since it's already after midnight."

Millie, seeing that Annette hadn't turned the knife on Cat, stepped closer. "Are we still on for our fact finding mission?"

Annette paused with the knife midair. "Of course! Now that Captain Vitale is on his deathbed, it's imperative we figure out who is out to get me."

Cat rolled up her sleeves. "Well, if we're going to get this mission under way in another hour, you'll need some help finishing this project."

Millie agreed. She headed to the sink to start scrubbing the mile high pile of dishes stacked inside.

An hour later, the girls had the kitchen spic and span. The ravioli was chilling in the fridge and the sauce was in large container right next to it. It would be an easy dish for Annette to assemble later that day. If they weren't taken into custody...

Millie glanced at her watch: 1:35 a.m. She swallowed the lump in her throat and followed Annette and Cat out of the kitchen. She reached behind her to turn off the light and close the door.

The ship was like a ghost town. If Millie had to guess, guests were in bed or closing down the bars, which is where Millie hoped the security staff was – far, far away from Deck 5 and Donovan's office.

She let out a sigh of relief that there was no one in sight.

Annette abruptly stopped in front of the guest service's counter. She motioned Millie ahead of her.

Millie sucked in a breath. *Here goes nothing.* She flung open the half door that separated the lobby from guest services before turning back. "Got your camera cover and phones?"

"Check." Annette nodded and thrust the tablecloth out for her to see. With one quick look back, the three of them tiptoed down the small hall.

Millie's hand shook as she lifted the lanyard from her neck and approached Donovan's door.

She whispered a small prayer. "Dear God, please protect us."

Millie shoved the card in the slot and waited for the familiar beep.

Annette squeezed past Millie and shoved the door open. She threw the cloth up at the camera that hung just above the door. It was a perfect throw and covered the camera completely.

The girls rushed in, cameras at the ready.

Annette grabbed a stack of papers and in one fell swoop, spread them out across the desk. Millie immediately started snapping pictures as quick as she could. Cat did the same while Annette kept an eye on the door.

"Eight seconds," Annette hissed.

Millie's hand shook. She was working so fast, she wasn't sure if she was getting clear shots or not. Either way, it would have to work. "I think I got them all."

"Me too," Cat said.

Annette gathered the papers, assembled them in a neat stack and shoved them back in the tray.

Cat bolted out the door first. Millie was right on her heels.

Annette was last. She reached up, grabbed the cloth that covered the camera and jerked the door shut behind her.

Millie's heart raced as they scurried through the half door that separated guest services from the lobby.

When they reached the lobby, the girls slowed their pace and nonchalantly strolled across the gleaming tile floor as they made their way down the stairs to the crew quarters.

No one spoke a word. Annette stopped in front of her cabin door, inserted her keycard and pushed the door open. The girls stepped inside.

Cat closed the door behind them.

Millie exhaled the breath she had been holding.

Annette rubbed her hands together. "Let's see what we've got."

Cat turned her camera to the "on" position and switched it to the picture screen then handed it to Annette.

Annette slipped her reading glasses on and slid her finger across the screen. "Cat, not a single one of these pictures turned out." She handed the phone back to Cat, who pulled the screen close and shook her head. "Oh no! I think I was so nervous my thumb got in the way!"

She dropped her hands in her lap. "I'm sorry, Annette."

"I took the same shots." Millie turned her phone on and scrolled to the pictures. She let out a sigh of relief. The first one appeared a bit blurry but at least she could see something. She handed the phone to Annette.

Annette studied the photos. "Hmm. I see a couple names I don't recognize." She lifted her head. "Is there any way to make the picture bigger?"

Millie nodded. She grabbed the phone, tapped the screen and handed it back.

Annette lifted it to her face. "Much better." She slowly shook her head. "Well, will you look at that?"

Cat and Millie leaned forward. "What?"

"I see Amit's application, Raj's application, Suri's application, and this last one. My, my, my, what a surprise..."

She looked up. Her eyes narrowed. "My little pal, Noel Kalani, applied for my job!"

Chapter 9

Millie wasn't surprised that Amit had applied or even Suri, but she was surprised at Noel's application. Noel was new and didn't strike Millie as having that go-getter, I'm-in-charge-and-the-boss personality.

"What about Veronica Chang?" That was the one Millie was putting her money on. There was something about that woman that didn't set right with Millie. Her radar went up every time she was around Veronica.

It was as if Veronica studied, dissected and somehow catalogued everyone she met as friend or foe.

Annette shook her head. "Nope. I don't see hers."

Millie frowned. That didn't necessarily clear her, but then it didn't really give the woman a motive, unless she just didn't like Annette for some reason.

Of course, maybe she had another strategy. Skip the kitchen and go right for Donovan, the man who controlled the money.

There was also the possibility that Millie had her all wrong.

"So now what?" Cat lifted her arms above her head and yawned. Her shirt became untucked and Millie caught a glimpse of the long, angry scar that ran from Cat's side and slashed across her abdomen.

Annette had told Millie not to mention the scar, but Millie couldn't help herself. "Cat, where on earth did you get such a horrible scar?"

Cat immediately dropped her arms and tugged at the bottom of her blouse. "Oh, that old thing."

"That is a serious scar," Millie said. "I mean, I don't want to be nosy but I guess I am."

Annette turned her gaze to Cat, curious to see what answer Cat would give.

Cat lifted her meticulously manicured nails as if to inspect them up close. She picked at the edge. "It was a parting gift from my ex-husband," she admitted.

Millie gasped. Her horrified gazed dropped to the scar, now hidden beneath the silky pink fabric.

Annette rose from the chair. She gently sat down on the other side of Cat. "Oh, dear."

"I've never told anyone about it," Cat confessed, "at least, not anyone here on the ship."

Millie placed a hand on her arm. "It's okay if you don't want to talk about it." She pointed at Annette. "We're your friends and we care about you, that's all."

Cat folded her hands in her lap. She gazed up at Millie, her eyes shined brightly. She sucked in a deep breath and closed her eyes. Two lone tears trickled down her cheeks. "I-I…"

Annette placed an arm around her shoulder. "Take your time."

Slowly, haltingly, Cat told them that as a love-struck teenager she had married, Rick, her high school sweetheart. They had been young and very much in love.

Rick had worked his way through college to become a police officer, something he was proud of but something that scared Cat to death.

To make ends meet, she waited tables at the only restaurant in their small town of Gunner. The couple had been married just over a year when Cat found out she was pregnant. Although money would be tight, the young couple was over the moon when they found out.

Cat sucked in a shaky breath. Her tears began to flow. Annette ducked into the bathroom and returned with a box of Kleenex. She handed a tissue to Cat and the girls waited for her to blow her nose.

"Rick worked nights. All of the rookies did. Anyways, one night after work, I came home and fixed supper. It was meatloaf, Rick's favorite. I remember putting it in the fridge with a note on top that said, 'I love you' and then went to bed."

Cat twisted the tissue between her fingers. "I fell right asleep. Of course, being pregnant I was exhausted all of the time."

Cat sucked in a deep, jagged breath. "I woke to the sound of someone pounding on the front door. I jumped out of bed and ran to the window. When I peeked through the curtains, I saw a patrol car and Rick's partner, Mike, standing out front. I knew right then that Rick was gone."

Millie felt tears burn the back of her eyes. She glanced over at Annette, tears streaming down her cheeks.

Cat leaned her head back and closed her eyes. Her voice was raw. "It's like it happened yesterday," she whispered.

Millie wondered about the baby.

"I lost the baby less than a week after I lost Rick. The stress and trauma of his death was too much," she said.

The girls sat in silence for a long time. Millie felt horrible that she had mentioned the scar. She wondered if the scar had something to do with the baby...

Cat lowered her head and stared blankly at the wall on the other side of the room. "For years I was an empty shell. I had lost the most important person in the world. I planned to spend the rest of my life alone. No one could replace Rick. No one."

"Then one day, about 12 years ago, I stopped by the car dealer in nearby Drayton to have my car repaired. That is where I met, Jay. He was charming. He was funny. I fell hard and fast." Cat shrugged. "After all of those years alone, I guess I was finally ready to let someone in my life again."

Cat abruptly stood and started to pace the floor. Back and forth. The tears were gone, replaced by anger.

"We married a few short weeks after we met. It was so romantic. We jetted off to Vegas and Elvis married us." She smiled wryly. "The honeymoon lasted about as long as the courtship."

Cat went on to tell the girls that for almost ten years, Jay physically and emotionally abused her. She explained how he would not allow her to work, that he rarely allowed her to even step outside their home and then it was only if Jay was with her.

"Jay began to drink hard liquor. He would stumble home most nights, too drunk even to walk. He called me a tramp and accused me of running around on him. I never did."

Cat took a deep breath and continued. "The beatings kept getting worse. The day he brought a gun home, I knew I had to find a way to escape, to disappear. He often threatened that if I ever tried to leave, he would track me down and kill me."

She laughed but it was hollow and emotionless. "I knew that even if I stayed he would kill me."

She stopped in the middle of the floor and turned to face her friends. "I waited too long. One night, he came home in a fit of rage like I'd never seen. I thought for sure he was going to shoot me but he didn't. Instead, he pulled a knife from the knife rack. The biggest one we had."

Cat started to pace again, her words tumbled from her lips. "I tried to escape. I made it as far as the front door. Jay grabbed a handful of my long hair and dragged me back into the kitchen."

"He threw me to the floor and plunged the knife into my side." Cat lifted her blouse and pointed to the edge of the scar. "He started here and sliced all the way across my stomach, all the while screaming at me to die. That I was nothing but a..."

Millie jumped from the bed and darted over to Cat. She wrapped her arms around her anguished friend. Cat sobbed for several long moments. Her sobs were painful and grief-filled ones that wracked her thin frame.

Annette came around the other side and the two women consoled Cat as a torrent of pent up emotions finally found an escape.

Cat's sobs subsided. She reached over, grabbed a tissue and dabbed at her eyes.

"When I came to, I was in the hospital. The doctors told me I almost died. Luckily, the neighbor in the apartment above us heard Jay screaming at me and called the police."

"As soon as they released me from the hospital, I hid out at a friend's house. I found the job for the cruise ship days later and knew this would be my only chance to get away from Jay.

That this would be a safe haven and that he would never find me here."

"Did he go to prison for attempted murder?" Millie hoped he had.

Cat nodded. "Yes. Believe it or not, he just got out." She balled the Kleenex in her hand. "I'm terrified he's going to track me down," Cat admitted.

Annette had a thought. "Can't the cruise line put him on some sort of blacklist?"

"Yeah," Cat said, "he's on a blacklist but you don't know Jay." She shuddered. "I know he's out there somewhere, looking for me right now."

"Is there anyone you know that can keep tabs on him?" Millie asked. "Surely there is someone who could give you a heads up if he's coming this way."

Cat slumped into the desk chair. "His sister, Susie. I kept in contact with her. That's how I found out that he's out of prison."

Millie crossed her arms. "She wouldn't rat you out, would she?"

Cat shook her head. "No way! There is no way Susie would tell him anything. The only reason she stays in contact with him is to let me know where he is."

Annette patted her shoulder. "Thank you for sharing that, Cat. I know it was hard."

Cat agreed. "It was hard but it's also a relief."

"Your secret is safe with us," Millie reassured her.

"I appreciate that. The only other person on board that knows anything is Donovan. I told him that I have a restraining order against my ex-husband for attempted murder."

Millie was curious. "Could Jay track you down by your last name?"

Cat chewed her lower lip. "Nope. I changed my name. Catherine Wellington is not my real name."

She went on. "My real name is Kate Bellinger, but I go by Cat."

Cat – or Kate – waved her arms in the air. "Enough about me and my sob stories. We need to get back to the real crisis...saving Annette's job!"

"So what's the plan?" Millie and Cat turned to Annette.

Annette settled back into the chair. "Our first step is to figure out who had contact with the lobster bisque between the time I tasted it and handed it off to Amit and the time Captain Vitale ate the first spoonful."

"It would also be helpful if we could figure out what kind of poison was in it," Millie added.

Annette grabbed a pad of paper and pen from the desk. She slipped her reading glasses on and began to write. "List of Suspects" and underlined the heading.

Amit's name made the top of the list.

Next, she wrote down Noel. Third was Suri's name.

Cat glanced over her shoulder. Her eyes narrowed. "Is there anyone else you can think of that has an axe to grind?"

Annette tapped the pen against the sheet of paper. "Hmm." She shook her head. "Nope!"

Millie yawned. "I'm whupped." She glanced at the watch on her wrist. "I have to be up and report to work at 6:00," she moaned.

Cat nodded. "Me, too. We better get going."

Annette walked them to the door. "What's the plan?"

Millie held out an index finger. "One, we talk to Noel, Suri and Amit. We need to follow the food to find out who had an opportunity to tamper with the dish."

"I'll do it," Annette volunteered.

Millie shook her head. "You're too close to this one, Annette. Better let me handle it."

113

Annette's face drooped. She knew Millie was right. "Okay."

Annette reached the cabin door first. She swung the door open and came face-to-face with Dave Patterson, head of security. "Just the girls I was looking for."

He gave them a stern look and waved his hand. "Follow me."

Chapter 10

Millie swallowed hard. She followed Patterson and the girls trailed behind her. She knew they'd been busted, but how?

The operation had gone off without a hitch. Millie was certain they hadn't been caught on camera.

Had someone spotted them as they snuck back out? That was the only thing she could think of.

This was exactly what she hoped wouldn't happen! Millie knew that out of any of them, she was in the hottest of the water, what with her having the key that let them into Donovan's office in the first place.

Her armpits grew damp and a trickle of sweat ran down the center of her back. Her steps dragged, as they got closer to Patterson's office. It was as if she was walking to her own execution.

Patterson inserted his key card. He stepped across the threshold and held the door open while the three women made their way inside.

Cat took the chair closest to the wall. Annette sat in the other chair. Millie stood.

She studied Patterson's face as he made his way around the desk and settled into his chair. His expression was grave as he clasped his hands, placed his index fingertips together and rested his chin on top.

He studied Cat's face, then Annette's and finally Millie's. Millie felt as if she were some sort of fascinating insect beneath a microscope...one Patterson was about to squash.

He took a deep breath and leaned forward. "Care to tell me what you ladies have been up to this evening?"

Cat went for a total cover-up. No way did she want to end up in the slammer again - not if she could help it! She patted her beehive. A move Millie recognized as a sure sign of nervousness.

"Oh, just helping Annette out in the kitchen with tomorrow's dinner."

That was true. They had done that, prior to the break-in...

Annette clamped her mouth in a tight line and shook her head. She wasn't about to show her hand. If Patterson had something, she wanted him to tell her what it was. Maybe he thought the girls had done something but didn't have proof...

The silence in the room was deafening. The only sound was the tick-tick-tick of the wall clock. It sounded to Millie like a ticking time bomb about to explode, which it may as well have been.

She took a deep breath. "Why do you ask?" Millie had always heard if you didn't want to answer a question, answer the question with a question.

Patterson turned those "I-can-melt-butter-with-my-baby-blue-eyes" on Millie and she nearly dissolved into a molten puddle.

She wondered if he knew what affect those mesmerizing eyes had on the opposite sex.

Patterson grabbed a nearby pen and tapped it on his desk. "Someone saw the three of you coming out of Donovan Sweeney's office a short time ago, which was about the same time that the camera in Donovan's office went blank for a few short seconds."

"Tick-tick-tick" went the time bomb.

"This is my fault!" Annette blurted out. "I talked Cat and Millie into sneaking into Donovan's office!"

Patterson turned an expressionless face to Annette. "Why did you break into Donovan's office?"

Millie didn't like how he used the word "break," as if they had committed a crime. "Sneak" sounded much better.

"Because someone is trying to throw Annette under the bus and make it look like she's poisoning the crew," Cat piped up.

"What does that have to do with Donovan?" Patterson asked.

"Because Annette's contract is up and Donovan has the applications. We thought that maybe someone that was gunning for her job was trying to sabotage the food and get her fired," Millie said.

Patterson nodded. "I see." He dropped the pen and leaned his elbows on the edge of the desk. "I'll get with Donovan later this morning. The incident will have to be reported."

The girls nodded in unison.

"Then what?" Cat asked.

Patterson rose to his feet. "It will be up to Donovan. He can either let it go with a warning. He could revoke Millie's card privileges."

Millie's heart sank. That would be a definite demotion.

"Last but not least, you could all be fired for knowingly violating company policy."

The girls somberly exited the small office single file and silently walked back to I-95 and the crew quarters. No one uttered a word as one-by-one they made their way to their cabins.

Millie didn't bother turning on the cabin lights. She was certain Sarah was sound asleep. Judging by the soft snores coming from the upper bunk, she was correct.

Millie slipped into the small bathroom and turned on the light. She leaned forward and peered in the mirror. She looked tired, which was to be expected since it was now the wee hours of the morning.

She brushed her teeth, splashed cold water on her face and changed into her pajamas. Millie crawled into bed and pulled the covers to her chin. She was so distraught at the thought of losing her job; she uttered just one small prayer before closing her eyes. "Lord, please don't let me lose my job."

***

It seemed as if Millie had just fallen asleep when the alarm went off and scared the dickens out of her.

Sarah rolled over in the top bunk and moaned.

Millie quickly shut the alarm off and slid out of bed. She shuffled to the bathroom and turned on the shower. The warm water soothed her skin, which made her feel a bit better.

She turned off the water and grabbed her towel. After she dried her body, she brushed her locks. Her hair seemed to have grown several inches since she started the job.

Millie dabbed foundation on her face and added a little mascara to her lashes. She stood upright and studied her reflection in the mirror.

She didn't look bad for having maybe three hours of sleep!

She slipped into a clean uniform before shutting off the light. She grabbed her lanyard from the hook near the door and eased out the cabin door, happy that she hadn't woken Sarah.

It was still early and the crew corridor was almost empty. Millie smiled at a couple of other crew as she made her way down the corridor and into the passenger area.

Today was turnaround day – the busiest day of the week. It was customary for Andy and her to meet bright and early on turnaround day since the cruise director was in charge of disembarkation. Not long after the last guest exited the ship, the new wave of passengers would start the boarding process.

Millie rounded the corner and entered Andy's small office. The first thing she noticed was Andy intently studying an array of papers spread out across his table.

The second thing she noticed was a carafe of coffee and two cups. "Bless your heart!" Millie slumped into a nearby seat and reached for a coffee cup.

Andy peered at her over the rim of his reading glasses. "I heard you had a little excitement last night."

Millie paused, her hand gripping the handle of the coffee cup. It never ceased to amaze her how quickly rumors spread around the ship! She grabbed the carafe and started to pour. "You heard about it already?"

"I ran into Patterson in the hall a few minutes ago. He was on his way to Donovan's office."

Millie frowned. She remembered the clock on Patterson's wall. *Tick-Tick-Tick.*

Andy removed his reading glasses and leaned back in his chair. "I love you, Millie. I love your enthusiasm. I love your sense of adventure. I love how you relate to the passengers. I'd hate to see you go."

He went on. "Sneaking into the purser's office may have crossed the line. Your fate is in Donovan's hands and there's nothing I can do."

Millie swallowed hard. She knew she could be a handful, that she had a penchant for ending up in sticky situations and that she had a tendency to bend the rules, but trouble was like a magnet to Millie and sometimes she was powerless to control herself.

"Just before you got here, Donovan radioed and asked that the two of us meet him in his office." Andy glanced down at his watch. "We have 15 minutes. I'll try to go to bat for you, but you need to tell me what happened and start at the beginning. The *very* beginning..."

Millie nodded. She took a deep breath and plunged into the story, starting with yesterday in the gym when Amit radioed Annette to let her know there was another possible food poisoning.

She told him that Annette's contract was up for renewal, and that several employees had applied for the position. She also explained how Donovan had told Annette it was against company policy to share any information about the applicants.

Andy interrupted. "Who are they?"

Millie sipped her coffee. "Amit, Suri and Noel, the new girl."

Andy nodded thoughtfully. "Hmm. Go on."

Then she told him how they hatched a plan to snap a few photos of the applications.

"So you used your keycard to sneak into Donovan's office, snap pictures of the applications and then sneak back out."

"Yep," Millie said. She liked how Andy used the word "sneak" instead of the words that Patterson had used earlier – "broke into."

"Someone saw us leave and reported it to Patterson," Millie said. She finished the last of her coffee and pushed the cup aside.

Andy shuffled the papers into a pile and stood. "Let's get this over with."

The two of them walked silently across the back of the stage, down the stairs and out of the theater.

Millie wondered if Cat and Annette would be there, too.

Andy led the way as they stepped behind the guest services desk. He knocked on Donovan's door.

"Come in."

Millie stepped into the room and locked eyes with Donovan Sweeney, the person who held her fate in his hands.

Chapter 11

Dave Patterson stood in the corner of the room while Donovan waved at the two empty seats in front of his desk.

Andy slumped into the chair while Millie sat on the edge of her seat, ready to bolt at a moment's notice.

Donovan glanced at Andy first and then his eyes traveled to Millie as he studied her intently. She wondered if he and Patterson had taken the same "make-your-prey-squirm" class.

She lifted her chin defiantly and stared into Donovan's eyes, refusing to blink.

Andy cleared his throat, clearly uncomfortable with the heavy silence in the room. "I explained to Millie why we're here."

Donovan nodded. "Do you have anything you'd like to say in your defense?"

At least Donovan was giving her a chance! "Only that we meant no harm," she answered truthfully, "and that I was trying to help Annette because someone is trying to get her fired," she added.

The room, once again, grew silent.

Millie's mind raced as a million different thoughts ping-ponged around in her head. She wondered if she would get a chance to tell Scout good-bye.

Dave Patterson broke the silence. "So what do you think, Donovan?"

Donovan drummed his fingers on the desk. His eyes met Millie's eyes. "I like you Millie." He pointed to Andy. "Andy adores you. He told me you are one of the best assistant cruise directors he has ever had."

Millie's face turned beet red. "I like him, too."

"The crew likes you. The passengers love you. Heck, even the captain has taken a shine to you."

If possible, Millie's face turned even redder.

"I think your heart was in the right place," he said, "so I propose a quasi-probation." He pointed to the lanyard around her neck. "We take away your special access to areas like the bridge and my office…"

"For how long?" Andy interrupted.

"Thirty days," Donovan said, "starting today." He held out his hand.

Millie lifted the lanyard from around her neck and dropped it into Donovan's outstretched hand.

Dave Patterson crossed his arms and rocked back on his heels. "That seems fair. What do you think, Millie?"

She nodded, not trusting herself to speak lest she burst into tears and embarrass herself even more than she already had.

Andy recognized the look. He reached over and patted her on the back as he tried to lighten the mood. "I'll try to keep her in line."

Donovan grinned.

Patterson grimaced. "Good luck with that one."

Even the corners of Millie's mouth turned up.

Andy stood. Millie took that as her cue and got to her feet. She was safe but now she was worried about her friends. "What about Annette and Cat?" she blurted out.

Andy grabbed the door handle. "They've been warned but they got off a bit lighter than you since you blatantly used a privilege to break a company policy."

Millie's shoulders sagged in relief. Annette and Cat were safe! They were all safe! Now it was on to figure out who was out to get Annette.

"Thanks, Donovan," she said gratefully.

Before she had a chance to stick her foot in her mouth, she made her way out into the guest services area.

The three men followed her to the desk where Donovan opened a drawer and pulled out a new keycard. He handed it to Millie. "This is your temporary ID for the next 30 days. If you stay out of trouble, you'll get your old one back."

Millie impulsively reached up and hugged Donovan. He stiffened and then relaxed as he hugged her back. "You sure do make things exciting around here," he admitted.

"I take back all those terrible things I said about you," she teased.

Millie grabbed the lanyard and dropped it around her neck. "So I can still work on Annette's investigation?"

Patterson winked one of his baby blues. "Yes. As long as you don't break company policy. Remember, you're on probation for thirty days."

Millie lifted her hand in a mock salute. "Yes, sir."

Donovan returned to his office; Patterson to check on customs and debarkation. Millie and Andy headed to the crew dining room to grab a quick bite to eat before supervising debarkation.

Millie followed Andy down the food line. This morning they actually had hot breakfast sandwiches, something Millie had never seen before. "I wonder what the special occasion is," Millie said.

Andy shrugged. "Never look a gift horse in the mouth."

"True."

The two of them wandered to an empty table. Millie set her tray on the table and pulled out the chair. "Have you heard how Captain Vitale is doing?"

Andy lifted the top of his English muffin, grabbed the saltshaker and sprinkled salt on top.

Sprinkled may have been too weak of a word. He dumped a ton of salt on his egg before replacing the top. "I'm not sure. I know they are pumping him full of fluids and he has already asked when he can come back."

"And?"

Andy lifted the sandwich and took a bite. "Hmm...not bad. Tastes like fast food."

Millie bit into her sandwich. He was right. It wasn't too shabby.

He dumped more salt on his hash browns before he answered. "He'll be out until at least next week when the new passengers get on."

That made sense to Millie. If he was so ill that they had to airlift him off the ship, he should take it easy for a few days. Maybe he could take a mini vacation, head to the beach and catch a few rays.

Andy gobbled his sandwich in record time. He reached for his napkin and wiped the corners of his mouth. "What happens next in the investigation?"

"We trace the lobster bisque; try to figure out who had access to the dish, and who delivered it to the officer's dining room."

"I'd start with Doctor Gundervan," Andy advised. "He was eating with Captain Vitale when it happened."

Millie frowned. Doctor Gundervan didn't care for Millie. At least she didn't think so - not since Millie's investigation into the Olivia LaShay murder, an employee who died onboard the ship. Millie had named him as one of her suspects.

After that incident, he gave Millie the cold shoulder.

Maybe she could send Cat down to talk to him, or even Annette.

"Good to know," Millie said. No sense telling Andy that Gundervan didn't like her.

He glanced at his watch. "It's almost show time."

Millie popped the last bite of sandwich in her mouth, downed the last sip of coffee and followed him out of the cafeteria.

Today was turning out to be a good day, after all. At least she still had a job!

***

Andy and Millie watched as security stood at the exit doors. Passengers used their key cards to swipe through a machine that tracked guests. Security was then able to tell when everyone had gotten off.

It looked as if, finally, the last guest had exited.

Andy and Millie turned to go when Patterson's voice hit the airwaves. "We have a problem."

Andy and Millie strode over to the podium. "What's going on?"

The security guard at the exit shook his head. "We have one passenger unaccounted for."

Andy ran a hand through his crew cut. "A stowaway?"

"It would appear so, Mr. Andy," the guard said. "We are checking the stateroom now."

The guard's radio squawked. "Oscar, are you there?"

Oscar pulled the radio from his belt, held it to his lips, and then pressed the button. "Go ahead."

"The room is clean."

"10-4." He clipped the radio to his belt and looked up.

Andy massaged the back of his neck. In all his years as cruise director, he had only dealt with stowaways two other times. One was a female guest who had hooked up with one of the crew and the crewmember had hidden the guest inside his cabin.

The other was a drunken passenger that had passed out in the sauna. They had searched the ship for hours and finally gave up.

He surfaced halfway to the Bahamas where the captain promptly kicked him off the ship and he had to find his own way back home.

Dave Patterson rubbed his temple. This was going to be a long day. "The first thing we need to do is assemble a search party, start on the top deck and work our way down. In the meantime, we station a crewmember at each of the stairwells."

Andy nodded. "Millie and I will head to the bridge to let the captain know, then join the search."

Patterson turned the button on his radio. "We have a DND. All security to the sky deck except for those assigned to the stairwells. Stat!"

Patterson clipped the radio to his belt. "Did not depart, or more proper name, disembark," he explained.

Andy and Millie quickened the pace as they made a fast track to the bridge.

Andy tapped on the door that led to the bridge, inserted his keycard and opened the door.

Captain Armati was standing at the wall of windows, a pair of binoculars pressed to his face. He lowered the binoculars when he saw Andy and Millie. "Is there a problem?"

Andy nodded. "We have one DND."

Captain set the binoculars on the stand and tucked his arms behind his back. "Security is searching the ship?"

"As we speak."

"Good, please keep me up-to-date."

Andy lifted his hand in salute. "Yes, sir."

Andy turned to go. The captain winked at Millie, and her face turned fire engine red.

Millie followed Andy as they made their way across the bridge when a thought occurred to her. She spun back around. "Can Scout come with us? He has a good sniffer. Maybe he can help."

Armati nodded. "Yes, of course." Andy and Millie waited while Captain Armati retrieved Scout. When he returned with pup in hand, he set Scout on the floor and handed Millie his leash. "Good luck."

The three of them exited the bridge and headed up the side stairs. This was turning out to be quite an exciting day! Millie had never searched for a missing passenger!

Chapter 12

By the time Andy and Millie made it to the top deck, the search party had already assembled off to the side of the Sky Bar.

Patterson strolled back and forth, his heavy footsteps echoed on the deck boards. "We need to search every nook and cranny of this ship. Leave no stone unturned. No toilet stall unchecked."

As he barked the orders, the loudspeakers began to call the passenger's name. Repeatedly. "William Kent, please contact guest services immediately."

The search party dispersed. Several headed to the chapel, others to the VIP area while still others made a beeline for the bathrooms near the bar.

Andy had his own plan. "We'll follow behind in a final sweep," he told Millie. "That way, if the passenger is trying to be sneaky and thinks the search crew has already gone through, he'll come out of hiding."

Millie admired the strategy.

The two of them waited until the search party descended to the next level before they started their own search.

The chapel was empty, the VIP area clean, behind the bar – no one. They did a final sweep of the sky deck, and then moved on. The crew had moved on, too, and were nowhere in sight.

Andy, Millie and Scout conducted a thorough search of every nook and cranny of the sun deck, including the spa and sauna.

By the time they got to Deck 7, they still hadn't seen a single trace of the missing passenger.

They started the search in the women's restroom, across from the second floor theater seating. One of the cleaning crew was inside and told them she hadn't seen anyone.

Millie started to have doubts. They were running out of common areas where the man could be hiding. "You don't suppose he went overboard last night?"

The muscles in Andy's jaw tightened. "Good heavens! I hope not!"

They stepped out of the restroom and crossed the hall to the men's restroom.

Andy opened the door and stepped inside. He held the door for Millie and Scout.

The stalls were empty – the cabinets locked. They turned to go when Scout stopped in the middle of the room and refused to budge.

"C'mon Scout," Millie coaxed.

Scout let out a low growl. His ears flattened.

Millie bent down. "What is it?"

Scout lowered his head to the ground and sniffed the tile floor. He tugged on his leash as he led Millie inside the handicapped stall and over to a large, square side panel in the corner. The panel was unhinged and tilted at an odd angle.

Millie and Scout slowly backed away from the stall.

Andy put a finger to his lips and tiptoed over to the panel. He bent down, stuck his finger on the corner and in one sharp movement, yanked the panel from the wall.

Out flopped a tennis shoe, then another.

"Come on out of there," Andy commanded in a stern voice.

Slowly, a young man, who looked to be in his mid-20's, wearing khaki shorts and a pale yellow striped shirt, emerged. A thin layer of dust clung to his hair and his clothes. "Achoo!"

"Bless you," Millie automatically replied.

Andy gave her a dark look.

Millie shrugged.

Andy grabbed the young man's arm. "I assume you are William Kent."

William Kent a/k/a dust bunny nodded.

Millie held the door as Andy and the errant traveler stepped out into the hall.

Millie snatched her radio from her belt and lifted it to her lips. "Patterson, do you copy?"

"Go ahead."

"We're on Deck 3 with the DND."

Millie could hear the relief in his voice. "10-4. I'll be right there."

Patterson must have been lurking in the vicinity, as he appeared just seconds later, looking more than a little ticked off.

Andy handed the passenger over. He and Millie watched as Patterson and Mr. Kent disappeared around the corner.

"Way to go, Scout!" Andy reached down and patted his head.

"Just for that, you get a special treat today," Millie promised.

"Woof!"

The three of them headed up to Deck 5. With all passengers accounted for, the ship could begin the boarding process.

Millie was certain the new wave of guests would be chomping at the bit. She was 100% correct. Moments later, Andy and she watched as hordes of passengers dashed up the glass enclosure, anxious to begin their vacation.

Millie studied the faces as they passed by and entered the atrium. None of them seemed too irate that they had been kept waiting. "They're all taking it quite well," she observed.

Andy nodded. "The guests were informed of the reason for the delay," he told her out of the corner of his mouth. "Maybe we should have turned Mr. Kent over to the passengers waiting to board," he joked.

They spent the next several hours greeting guests, answering questions and directing them to lunch on the lido deck. Millie's back ached and her feet started to throb. Finally, security pulled the entrance door closed and the ship was on its way.

Millie and Scout headed to the top deck to check on the sail away party while Andy headed to the bridge to give the captain a full report on the stowaway incident and to tell him what a great job Scout had done.

The party was well under way and guests were having a grand time. School had started for most of the youngsters so there weren't as many pint size passengers onboard.

Millie made a note to talk to Andy about helping out in the children's area. She missed her grandkids and spending time with the youngsters might help with her homesickness. Plus, Scout would be a hit with the children onboard.

Millie grabbed a slice of pizza from the pizza station and wandered to a quiet table in the rear. Cat was there and must have had the exact same thought. She motioned Millie over.

"Whew! That was a close call this morning," she said as Millie slid into a bench seat. Scout settled onto her lap and she fed him small bits of pizza while she ate.

"No kidding." Millie shuddered.

"You met with Donovan?" Cat picked up her burger and took a bite.

Millie nodded and flicked the lanyard that hung around her neck with the tip of her fingers. "Probation."

Cat arched a brow. "Oh no. They took your access card?"

"Yep." Millie popped a pepperoni in her mouth. "Thirty days limited access. If I behave myself I'll get my card back next month."

Cat lifted her straw and used the tip to stab the ice cubes in her glass. "What about the investigation?"

Millie swallowed a bite of pizza. "They didn't say anything about that."

She went on. "I found out that Doctor Gundervan was in the dining room with Captain Vitale when the lobster bisque arrived." Millie poured some water in her cupped hand and held it for Scout to drink.

"Oh," Cat's expression brightened, "that's helpful."

Millie nodded. "So someone needs to talk to him but not me. He doesn't like me."

Cat lifted her glass and sipped her tea. "Why not?"

"The Olivia LaShay investigation."

Cat snorted. "So you stepped on Gundervan's toes, too?"

"You could say that." Millie finished her pizza and picked up her napkin to wipe her lips. "So that leaves you to talk to him since he doesn't like me and Annette is too close to the investigation."

"Great. I've never gone solo. What should I say? What excuse do I use?"

Millie stared out the window at the water, the wheels in her head spinning as she thought of some excuse. Her eyes turned to focus on Cat. "Well, you could tell him you think you have food poisoning."

"Uh-uh." Cat stiffened her back and shook her head. "No way. If he thinks I have food poisoning or even worse, the Norovirus, he'll put me in quarantine."

True. Millie hadn't thought about that. "What about an allergic reaction? Then you can steer the conversation towards the bisque. You know, kind of bring it up while you're talking."

"True..." Cat appreciated the fact that Millie trusted her enough to go it alone in the investigation, but what if she bombed? What if Gundervan caught onto her?

Millie read her mind. "Look, the worst thing that can happen is he calls your bluff. I mean, it's not like he can fire you or anything."

"Okay." Cat finished her tea and set the empty glass on her tray. "I'll do it!"

"Good girl," Millie encouraged. "Now see what you can find out!"

Chapter 13

Cat glanced at her watch nervously. She had twenty minutes before it was time to open the gift shop. As she walked, she rehearsed what she would say to Doctor Gundervan.

She tried to remember everything she knew about food allergy symptoms: hives, rash, itching...

Cat stopped in front of the infirmary door and tapped on the frosted glass. No one answered. She tried again, this time a little louder. There was still no answer.

She put her hand on the knob and turned. The door was unlocked!

Cat slowly pushed the door open and stepped inside. She could hear faint rustling coming from somewhere in the back.

She cleared her throat. "Ahem."

The rustling continued.

"Hello? Anyone here?"

The rustling stopped. "Be right out," a male voice answered.

Cat tugged at the side of her skirt to wiggle it down. She stepped over to the wall and studied the plaque. It was Doctor Gundervan's medical license. *Joseph Gundervan.*

"Can I help you?"

Cat whirled around, her face warmed. "I-I."

Doctor Gundervan was young. Younger than Cat had assumed he was. Not that she had ever met him. In fact, she had only seen him briefly here and there and never up close. He was handsome, with sandy brown hair and smokin', gray eyes. *Hottie.*

Cat sucked in a breath. "I ate some peanut butter this morning and now I feel all itchy." She scratched the side of her stomach for emphasis.

"Hmm." A concerned look crossed Gundervan's face. "Any other symptoms?"

Cat's hand flew to her throat. "Yeah, my throat feels kinda swollen and scratchy."

Gundervan pointed at her stomach. "Mind if I take a look?"

The color drained from Cat's face. *Why on earth had she said her stomach itched?*

"Well-uh."

He smiled. "Just a quick peek..."

Cat didn't know how to say "no." She lifted the edge of her shirt and squeezed her eyes shut. *Please don't mention the scar!*

Doctor Gundervan leaned in for a closer look. If he noticed the long, angry scar, which Cat was one thousand times certain he had...how could he miss it? He didn't say anything.

"I see a couple small bumps but otherwise, you're clear as a bell," he said.

Doctor Gundervan reached inside his pocket and retrieved a small penlight. "Open your mouth, stick out your tongue and say 'ah.'"

"Ah."

He peered inside then clicked the penlight off. "That looks fine, too."

Gundervan opened the cabinet door next to him and pulled out a small packet of pills. He held them out. "Here are some allergy tablets. If your symptoms worsen or start to bother you, take one of these. They won't hurt you."

Cat took the tablets and shoved them in her front pocket. "Thank you. I'll be sure to keep them handy."

She turned to go and then turned back. "Say...I heard you were with Captain Vitale when he ate the lobster bisque."

Gundervan closed the cabinet drawer. "Yes. He grew ill almost immediately." Gundervan cocked his head to the side. "That is a little odd. Typically, food poisoning takes a little longer to affect the body. His was almost instantaneous."

"Maybe it wasn't food poisoning, after all," Cat theorized.

Gundervan nodded. "I have my suspicions. I asked for a copy of the lab's findings and am waiting to hear back. I guess it's a good thing I'm not a fan of lobster."

Cat leaned in. "Do you know who it was that delivered the dish to your table?"

Gundervan shook his head. "Unfortunately, no. I had gone into the restroom to wash my hands. When I returned, the dish was already on the table."

That meant that only Captain Vitale knew who dropped the food off!

Cat smiled. She patted her pocket. "Thanks again for the tablets. I'm feeling much better now," she added.

Gundervan followed Cat to the outer office door. She almost made it out the door without the prodding, probing questions about her scar.

Almost, but not quite. "That's a nasty scar on your abdomen."

Cat shifted her feet and stared down at the floor. "Yes, it is."

"Sometimes old scars flare up and cause pain. If it ever starts to bother you, stop by and I'll see what I can do," he said kindly.

Cat smiled. "Thank you. So far, so good, except when I try to stretch too far it starts to pull and I get sharp shooting pains."

He nodded. "That's normal."

Cat stepped out of the office and started down the hall. She decided he was a nice man and wondered if maybe Millie had Doctor Gundervan pegged all wrong.

Cat made it to the gift shop with a couple minutes to spare. Several guests were milling about, waiting for her to unlock the doors. The guests followed Cat into the shop and that was the last thought she had of the nice doctor.

***

Annette was in the midst of conducting an investigation of her own. Well, perhaps it was more like an interrogation – of poor Amit.

"I handed you the pot of lobster bisque and where did you take it from there?"

"I told you, Miss Annette. I headed for the door to take it directly to the officer's dining room. I ran into Suri who told me *he* was on his way to the same place and offered to take the bisque for me."

"Then what happened?" she asked.

Amit shrugged. "Suri headed to the door with the bisque and another dish and I went back to the pastry station to help out."

"To help Noel?" Annette prompted.

Amit hung his head. "Yes, to help Noel. She was falling behind in her pastry filling so I offered to help."

"Did you see Suri when he came back after he supposedly delivered the dish?"

Amit shook his head. "No. I never saw him come back and it wasn't until later, until after Captain Vitale became ill that I discovered Suri had left the pot in the warming bay and someone else picked it up."

Annette shoved a hand on her hip. "As of right now, we don't know who delivered the bisque to the dining room."

Amit shook his head. "No, Miss Annette." More than anything, Annette wanted to confront Amit about submitting his application but she didn't dare. She wasn't supposed to know and she had promised Donovan she wouldn't spill the beans. That was part of the deal the girls had agreed to, and it was how she and Cat had gotten off the hook, so to speak.

Millie had stopped by a short time ago to tell her Cat was in Gundervan's office fishing for information. Annette hoped she was having more luck than she herself was.

Maybe she could take a quick break after the desserts left the kitchen, and sneak up to see what Cat was able to find out.

Annette turned her attention to the trays of ravioli that were ready to plate. She joined the end of the long line of prep staff and picked up a spoon.

Grace rushed into the prep area. "There's a fire behind the stove!"

Annette grabbed the fire extinguisher and bolted across the room. *Was this day ever going to end?*

Chapter 14

Annette quickly doused the small fire, caused by bacon grease that splattered a stack of paper towels nearby and then torched by a gas burner.

The dinner service finally ended, all of the dishes washed and leftover food refrigerated. Annette reached behind her back and untied her apron. She felt every day of her 61 years.

She had barely gotten a wink of sleep the night before. Dave Patterson had rudely awoken her when he started pounding on her cabin door before the sun was up. She and Cat ended up in Donovan's office, certain this was the end.

Surprisingly, Donovan was calm, cool and collected. He had not seemed angry. If anything, Annette sensed a deep disappointment, which was almost worse than anger.

The girls promised to stop the shenanigans. They also promised not to breathe a word of who had applied for Annette's job. What Donovan didn't make her promise was to halt the investigation.

Annette hung her apron on the hook by the door, turned off the light and stepped out of the kitchen. Her brain was fuzzy and for a moment, she couldn't remember what she was going to do before heading to her cabin for some much-needed rest.

Cat. She needed to talk to Cat. Annette glanced down at her watch: 10:05. The gift shop closed at 10:00. She hoped Cat was still there.

When Annette got to the gift shop, she could see the lights were still on and the tip of Cat's beehive hairdo bobbed up and down behind the counter.

She tried the door handle. Locked. She tapped lightly on the glass. Cat's head popped up. She grinned and walked over to the door to let Annette in.

Annette stepped across the threshold and Cat locked the door behind them. "Millie said you talked to Doctor Gundervan."

Cat nodded. "Yeah."

"And?" Annette prompted.

Before she could answer, there was another light tap on the door. This time it was Millie.

Cat let her in, locked the door, once again, and wandered to the back. "What did you find out?"

Cat tucked a wisp of jet black hair behind her ear. "I was just about to tell Annette that, although Doctor Gundervan was with Captain Vitale when he was poisoned, he didn't see who delivered the food. He had gone to the restroom to wash his hands and when he returned, the bisque was already on the table."

Annette's heart sank. "So Vitale is the only one who can tell us who dropped off the dish?"

Cat nodded. "Yep, but Doctor Gundervan did say something I thought was interesting."

Millie leaned in. Maybe they were finally going to get a break in the case. "What?"

"That Captain Vitale became violently ill almost immediately after eating the food. You know, food poisoning takes a little while to get into the system."

Annette nodded. "True. So what does he think it was?"

Cat shrugged. "He wasn't certain but he did say he was waiting on the lab results. He should have them any time now."

Annette's blue eyes gleamed with interest. "We need to get our hands on a copy of those results!"

Millie took a step back. She raised her hands. "Oh no...don't look at me! I'm already on probation."

Annette turned to Cat. "Think you can make up another excuse to get into Gundervan's office, maybe snoop around?"

163

Cat wiped a microscopic speck of dust off the cash register keys. "Maybe," she said.

Annette took that as a yes. "Good. We'll wait a couple days, then you go back down there to see what you can find out."

She went on. "In the meantime, I'll do a little research on the computer to see what kind of poisons or drugs would make someone ill almost immediately." Annette turned to Millie. "I'm not having much luck getting information out of my kitchen staff."

Millie had a hunch as to why that was the case. When Annette was onto something, she was like a bulldog. Sometimes you could attract more bees with honey than with vinegar.

Perhaps Millie could use a little honey... "I'll see what I can find out," she promised Annette, "but for now, I am exhausted."

The girls wandered out of the gift shop. Cat turned off the light and locked the door.

Back in her cabin, Millie stripped off her work clothes and slipped into her pajamas. She could barely keep her eyes open as she washed her face and brushed her teeth.

She crawled into her bunk, closed her eyes and was out like a light!

Millie dreamed she was in a small fishing boat. The boat bobbed up and down in the water, tossing and turning in the waves. Every time she tried to move around, another huge wave would hit the side of the boat and water poured over the top.

Millie's heart began to pound. Her stomach began to churn and she felt sick to her stomach.

She peered over the edge of the boat. When the small boat crested a wave, she could see a spot of land off in the distance. The small boat would dip back inside the enormous wave and the shoreline would disappear.

Millie began to pray, *"Dear God, please save me! I'm going to die!"*

The rain began to pelt her face, her body. A loud rumble of thunder and bolt of lightning struck nearby.

"Millie!" Someone outside the boat was calling her name.

"Millie! Wake up!"

Millie's eyes flew open.

Sarah was leaning over her, gently shaking her arm. "Are you okay? You were thrashing around in the bed, mumbling."

Millie propped herself on her elbows. "I was having a dream that..."

Suddenly, the cabin tilted. Millie's radio slid off the desk and hit the floor with a loud *thud*.

Sarah reached up and grabbed the edge of the top bunk to steady herself. "The ship is rocking and rolling. I'm about to head topside to see what's going on."

Millie flung the covers back and swung her legs over the side of the bed. "Wait for a minute and I'll go with you."

She stood up at the precise moment the ship tilted again. Like a drunken sailor, Millie stumbled to the bathroom.

She slipped into her uniform from the night before, smoothed her hair back in a quick ponytail and brushed her teeth.

All the while, the ship swayed back and forth. It started to make Millie feel a bit queasy.

Back in the main cabin, Sarah sat on the edge of Millie's bed. She looked as green as Millie felt.

Millie kept a package of mints in her dresser drawer for just such an emergency after Annette had urged her to keep them on hand.

She handed one to Sarah, peeled the wrapper off a second one and popped it into her mouth. Millie slipped her lanyard around her neck and grabbed the cabin door.

The two women weren't the only ones making their way to the upper decks to see what was going on. Several of the crew, looking bleary-eyed and leaning against the wall to steady themselves, made their way to the door that connected the crew quarters to the guest area.

The ship continued to rock and roll as the girls and several others climbed the stairs. Millie glanced at a cluster of passengers who held onto the wall and waited for an elevator.

Millie scrunched her brows. No way would she take an elevator with the ship shifting to and fro. Not that she would take an elevator, anyway. They were Millie's nemesis – at least one of them was.

Sarah and Millie stopped climbing when they reached the lido deck. They made their way through the sliding glass doors that separated the hallway and the pool area.

Water sloshed over the sides of the pool and spilled onto the teak boards. A net covered the pool. Millie grimaced. *Was someone actually crazy enough to jump in the pool in this storm?*

Rain pelted the open area and coated the deck. Awesome...a poolside slip and slide. The girls shuffled along the edge, staying just under the covered section as they made their way over to the wall of windows.

Even from the upper deck, Millie could see huge waves crash against the side of the ship. She lifted her gaze and focused on the horizon. The ship was to dock in Nassau, Bahamas today.

Through the haze of the storm, she could barely make out land and the outline of the luxurious resort, Atlantis, off in the distance.

One of the crew stood next to Sarah. She gave him a quick look. "We aren't going to dock." It wasn't really a question but more of a statement.

He shook his head. "No. It's too dangerous. I heard that the captain is deciding whether to wait out the storm or turn around and try to sail out of it."

Millie nodded. That made sense. She wondered how long the storm was supposed to last.

A towering wall of waves crashed against the windows. The ship groaned against Mother Nature's onslaught.

Millie grabbed the handrail in front of her to steady herself. She closed her eyes and willed the churning in her stomach to stop.

Closing her eyes made it worse so she opened them back up.

"Get ready for the barf bags." Millie gingerly turned. It was Zack.

She shot him a look. Barf bags? Millie had seen them before and had even asked Andy if they ever actually used them.

Andy told her that they did and even assured her that one day she would experience the rough seas.

"This is going to be a bad one," Zack predicted.

Sarah tightened her grip on the rail, her knuckles turned white. "Why do you say that?"

He shrugged. "Because I just saw some of the crew making their way down the corridors of the passenger cabins. They were shoving barf bags under each of the doors."

He turned to face Millie and she could see that even his face was quite pale. Zack was a seasoned cruiser and had probably experienced more than his share of stormy seas.

"I've only seen them do that one other time and it was a whopper of a storm that we got caught in. It was the time we skirted a Category 2 hurricane on our way to Mexico."

"So what should we expect?" Millie was nervous. She herself felt ill and wondered how much help she would be to the passengers. On top of that, Millie had a weak stomach and the sight of someone losing his or her cookies made her queasy. Even when her kids were young, she had a hard time.

"As far as your schedule today, you'll have to check with Andy," Zack replied. "He's down in his office."

Millie glanced at her watch. She didn't have to check in for another hour. Of course, the plan had been to meet Andy at the gangway to help passengers disembark in Nassau and answer any questions they may have.

It didn't look like that would happen. "Have you heard a weather report? Do we know how long this storm will last?"

Zack turned to face the angry seas. "As of right now, we're sitting right in the middle of it."

Millie wasn't surprised. She felt as if she was in one of those water globes with a small boat inside of it. One someone was violently shaking.

"I heard the captain is going to give it another hour to see if the storm starts to pass."

Sarah chimed in. "Does that mean we might dock in Nassau after all?"

Zack shook his head. "I'd bet money that the answer is no. These seas will be rough for at least the rest of today, if not longer. There's no way they can get the ship into port without chancing a run in with one of those long, cement pylons."

"So we'll wait out the storm and then head to South Seas Cay?" South Seas Cay was Majestic Cruise Line's private island. It was their next port stop, scheduled for the day after tomorrow.

Zack shrugged. "I have no idea. There's a chance the ship will head to Jamaica, then hit the private island on the way back if it's too rough."

That made sense to Millie. If the waters near the small island were as rough as they were right now, there was no way the shuttle boats could pull up next to the ship and transport passengers to shore. She wished she knew which way the storm was heading!

The girls started back to their cabin to get ready for work. Sarah, who worked in the dining room, clearing tables and helping with the buffet area, might have an easy day. If the passengers felt half as bad as Millie did, then they probably wouldn't be hungry.

Millie stepped between two bistro tables as she swaggered back and forth toward the sliding doors.

The poolside bar was packed. Millie stared in disbelief when she saw how many passengers were sitting at the bar, cocktail in hand. She looked at her watch again. It was only 6:30 in the morning!

Zack caught the look. "Believe it or not, a small drink can help with motion sickness, although after one, I'm not sure how much it helps."

Back inside, the trio headed down the steps. The ship continued to creak and groan at the onslaught of the massive storm. Millie said a quick prayer for their safety.

Millie followed Sarah into the cabin. "You can get ready first," she told her.

Millie grabbed the remote from the desktop and turned the TV on. The captain was on the screen. Millie turned the volume up.

"Good morning ladies and gentlemen. I am sorry to inform you that we have had to cancel our port stop in Nassau today. The ship has run into an unexpected storm and we cannot safely dock at this time."

He went on. "Due to the nature and length of the storm, I have decided to change course. Even now, the ship has turned and we are heading south towards South Seas Cay, our private island. Depending on weather improvement, we will either stop at the island tomorrow or continue on to Jamaica and stop at the private island on the way back."

Zack was good at calling it. Of course, he had a lot more experience at this than Millie did.

Sarah emerged from the bathroom moments later. Her face was not quite as pale. "That mint really helped. Do you mind if I take a couple more with me?”

"Of course not!" Millie reached into the dresser drawer and pulled the bag of mints. "Take as many as you want.”

"Thanks, Millie." Sarah dropped several mints in her pocket and eased onto the edge of the bed to slip into her shoes. "Good luck today."

"Same to you," Millie told her. "Save some saltines for me." She had heard that not only mints were good for settling the stomach but saltines helped, too.

Inside the bathroom, Millie hurriedly showered. The movement of the ship and the small, enclosed shower caused the queasiness to return with a vengeance.

She slipped into a clean uniform, opting to wear her sturdy black work shoes since they had more traction than her dressier work shoes.

After a quick inspection in the mirror, Millie turned off the lights and headed out into the hall. It was time to start her day.

Chapter 15

Millie made her way down the center aisle of the darkened theater. She gripped the edge of the theater chairs to steady herself as she walked. The sound of tinkling glass echoed in the empty, cavernous theater.

Millie lifted her eyes toward the ceiling. The mammoth crystal chandeliers swayed back and forth. Scenes from the movie *Titanic* ran through her head...would the ship capsize? *What if it took on water and sank to the bottom of the ocean?*

Millie had complete faith in Captain Armati, but even he might not be able to pull them through this one!

Millie stumbled to the stage and toward the bright light shining out from Andy's office.

Her heart plummeted when she caught a glimpse of her boss. He sat motionless, his face down, his head resting on his arms.

"Are you alright?"

"No," Andy moaned. He slowly lifted his head.

Millie glanced down at the large, rectangular trash bin sitting next to him. Several used barf bags filled the bin.

"I don't know what's wrong with me. I have never felt this sick before," he whispered.

Andy snatched an open bag from the table, spun around in his chair, lowered his head and filled the bag.

Millie scrunched her nose and tried to focus her mind elsewhere.

Andy turned back. "I need you to cover for me, Millie."

Millie's eyes widened. Those were some big shoes to fill. Of course, Millie was Andy's right-hand woman but she had never taken his place. Still, there was no way she could say "no." Andy had done so much for her.

"Of course. You go back to bed," she told him. "I'll handle everything."

Terrified, Millie plastered a smile on her face.

Andy struggled to get out of his chair. He took a step forward and lost his footing as he stumbled forward, tripping over his own feet.

Millie raced around the table. "Here, let me help you back to your cabin." She lifted Andy's arm and tucked her shoulder underneath. The two of them slowly made their way across the stage, down the stairs and out of the theater.

It was a long, slow journey to Andy's cabin. Millie took his key card and opened his cabin door. She helped him to his bed where he flopped down, flung his arm across his face and closed his eyes.

Andy's cabin was a bit larger and more luxurious than the rest of the crews' rooms. It even included a mini fridge.

Millie opened the refrigerator door. Her eyes scanned the interior as she searched the shelves.

She grabbed one of the water bottles and unscrewed the cap. "Here, drink this before you sleep." He needed to drink a lot of fluids or risk dehydration. The last thing she needed was for him to end up on a medevac and airlifted from the ship. Then she really would be up a creek without a paddle, floundering like a fish in a storm, literally!

Andy shifted to a sitting position. He took the bottle of water from Millie's hand. He gulped half the bottle, wiped his mouth with the back of his hand and handed it to her. "Thanks!"

He dropped his head on the bed and closed his eyes.

Millie placed the bottle on the nightstand. Next, she set Andy's radio on the other side of the water and then moved an empty trashcan close to the bed.

Millie slipped out the door, turning the light off as she went out. "Please, God. Heal Andy from whatever is making him ill and if it's the rough seas, please protect me from getting sick, too."

Millie quickened her pace and power-walked down the long I-95 corridor to the exit door. She headed straight to the theater and behind the stage.

The back area bustled with activity. Millie marched into the room. She breathed a sigh of relief to see that most of the dancers were milling about. "I need your help!"

All eyes turned to Millie. The room grew silent.

"Andy is sick. I just left him in his cabin. He put me in charge of entertainment and I can't do it all by myself," she said.

Alison, one of the dancers, stepped forward. "Of course, Millie. We'll do whatever we can to help."

Tears of relief burned the back of Millie's eyes.

Zack was there. He stepped next to Alison. "I can't believe Andy's sick. He was fine earlier. I've never seen him become ill from the motion of the ship. The man has a stomach of steel."

He sure didn't have a stomach of steel at the moment.

"Maybe he ate something for breakfast that caused it," Alison theorized.

Millie didn't have time to dwell on it now. She needed to rally the troops, form a plan, entertain the guests – what few of them that would be out and about.

If there was any saving grace, it was the fact that many of the passengers would hang out in their cabin...not that Millie wanted anyone to be ill.

"Let's head to Andy's office." Millie waved her hand and the group followed single file.

Millie sat in Andy's chair and the rest took up the empty seats. She slipped on her reading glasses and pulled Andy's notebook – his daily planner for ship activities – in front of her. She could see that Andy had started the revised schedule and made it as far as 11:00 a.m.

- 7:30 a.m. – Sunrise Stretch, Fitness Center
- 8:00 a.m. – Zoom with Zumba, Fitness Center
- 8:30 a.m. – Acupuncture Seminar
- 9:00 a.m. – Spirits and Samplers in Paradise Lounge. Millie wondered how anyone could drink with the tossing and turning of the ship, then she remembered the people up at the bar before it was even daylight.
- 10:00 a.m. – Acupuncture. How to relieve stress. Midship bar. Millie could use that class right about now!

The schedule ended there. Millie tapped her pen on top of the notepad. "I have a schedule that ends at ten. We can use parts of the schedule that was already printed but that schedule was based on a port day and outdoor activities."

Tara Daughtery, one of the other dancers, nodded. "When we have a cancelled port day or inclement weather, Andy revises the schedule, takes it down to the office and has copies printed. Someone from guest services arranges to have them dropped off at all the cabins."

Terror struck Millie's heart. Now, not only would she have to revamp the schedule, she would have to hurry up, get it printed and distribute it ship-wide. Her eyelid began to twitch.

Zack recognized her look of terror. "Don't worry, Millie. We'll help get the schedule up and running and make sure it all goes off without a hitch."

Millie turned grateful eyes to her young friend. "Thank you." She looked around the table. "Thank you all. I owe you one."

Millie rolled up her sleeves, determined to get the job done. Soon, they had a new schedule that would make Andy proud!

Millie jotted down the final activity and jumped from her seat. "Better get this puppy printed."

The group followed her out. "Make sure you tell them to drop them off in the cabins," Alison called after her.

Millie waved the papers in her hand. "Got it!"

Guest services was empty. Only a couple brave passengers milled about.

Millie stepped behind the door that separated the lobby from the back of the counter.

Nikki, Sarah's friend, was behind the desk. Millie handed her the sheets. "I need to get copies of this printed. It's the revised schedule."

Nikki nodded. "Great! We wondered when we would have it. Hang tight!"

She disappeared behind the doors in the back.

Donovan stepped out of his office and approached the counter. "What happened to Andy?"

Millie shook her head. "He's in bed, sicker than a dog. Looks like I'm in charge."

"You can handle it, Millie." He sounded a lot more confident than Millie felt. "I've never known Andy to get seasick – ever – and I've worked with him for years."

Nikki was back with a stack of the newly printed schedule of activities: *Cruise Ship Chronicles*. She handed a dozen to Millie. "The rest are headed to room stewards on each floor to leave under the door of every cabin."

Millie thanked Nikki and headed back to the theater. Her next task would be to decide who would host what events. The ship was still rocking and rolling and the halls still empty.

Either Millie was starting to get used to the rocking of the ship or the seas had started to calm. She hoped it was the latter. She wondered how Andy was doing and thought about what Donovan had said – that Andy had a strong stomach and he wasn't prone to motion sickness.

Maybe it was something else - *what if someone had poisoned Andy?*

Chapter 16

The entertainment staff was like angels, minus the wings. Whatever Millie asked them to do, they took the task with nary a grumble. When the meeting ended, they all split up and headed to their assigned activity.

The group was so helpful and so efficient that Millie had nothing to do! She wandered upstairs to the buffet area, which was virtually empty. Only a handful of passengers with strong stomachs were eating. They had the place to themselves.

Millie grabbed a plate and started down the buffet line. Even though her stomach was no longer queasy, she didn't dare push it. She settled for a scoop of scrambled eggs, a small pile of hash browns, some dry toast and an apple.

When she rounded the corner and started for the coffee station, she ran smack dab into Sarah, her roommate. Sarah looked down at Millie's plate. "You're feeling better," she observed.

Millie nodded. "I feel good but Andy..." She blew air through her thin lips, "he's sicker than a dog."

Sarah wiped her rag along the stainless steel cabinet and the puddles of spilled coffee disappeared. "Most of the guests are hanging out in their cabins." Sarah rolled her eyes. "Room service has gone berserk."

Millie hadn't thought about that. She hoped they wouldn't run out of saltine crackers and dry toast!

Sarah lifted the rag and folded it in her hand. "That and the bars are busier than ever."

Always one to look on the bright side, Millie was glad she didn't work for room service – or work at one of the bars. No, Millie was quite content to keep her own job!

She wandered to a table in the corner and slid into a booth that faced the window. The waves still looked huge. She shifted her gaze. Far off in the distance, she could see a faint line of clear skies. It looked as if calm seas were on the horizon!

After Millie finished her food, she dropped the dirty plates in the bin near the door and stepped out onto the lido deck.

The safety net still covered the entire surface of the pool. What was left of the water in the pool sloshed over the sides. She made her way across the lido deck and down to the kitchen.

By now, Annette would be hard at work and Millie wanted to talk to her about Andy. Now that she had a breather, she had time to think about how sick he had become.

Millie stepped into the kitchen, which was a beehive of activity. Staff bustled frantically here and there. They were right in the throes of the breakfast crunch.

She waited off to one side until she caught sight of Annette as she whizzed by on her way to the walk-in freezer. She held up a finger when she saw Millie.

A few minutes later, Annette made her way over to Millie. "This place is an absolute zoo. Room service, room service, room service. That, and barf bags."

Millie chuckled. "I heard it was bad."

Annette picked up a room service menu and started to fan herself. "This is as bad as I've ever seen it."

Millie wiped her brow. The kitchen was a bit on the warm side. "Speaking of bad, Andy is in his cabin. He became violently ill."

Annette dropped the menu. "Andy? That man has a gut of iron. Nothing makes him sick. In fact, I don't think I ever recall him getting sick."

Millie leaned in and lowered her voice. "He was throwing up. I had to help him to his cabin."

"You don't think…" Annette trailed off.

"Did he come up here to get a bite to eat or did you deliver food to him today?"

Annette's eyes shifted as she thought about it. The morning had been crazy. Even so, she would have remembered seeing Andy or sending food out of the kitchen. She could count on one hand how many times he had made a special request for meals and only in emergencies. "Nope. Not at all."

"When I leave here, I'm going to go check on him."

"Annette! We ran out of wheat bread!"

"I gotta run!" Annette darted off to the other side of the kitchen.

Millie headed out of the kitchen and straight to Andy's cabin. She tilted her head and placed her ear to the door. *What if he was asleep?*

Millie knocked softly and waited.

193

Slowly, the door opened and Andy peeked through the crack in the door. When he saw Millie, he opened it wider so that she could step inside.

Andy looked rough. His carefully groomed red hair stood straight up. A day's beard shaded his face. He was wearing a pair of boxer shorts, which Millie pretended not to notice, and a t-shirt covered with stains Millie did not want to dwell on.

"How are you feeling?" she asked.

Andy slowly lowered himself onto the edge of his bed. "Like I've been run over by a freight train carrying toxic chemicals and after the train ran over the top of me, my neck got caught on the caboose and it dragged me along a set of tracks with spiked rails for several miles."

"That bad?"

Andy rubbed his forehead. "No. Worse...much worse."

"I stopped by to check on you and to let you know that the backstage staff and I have everything under control so you stay here and rest."

Andy was visibly relieved. "Thank you, Millie."

"You're welcome," she told him. "Is there anything I can bring you? Soup? Toast?"

"No. If I get hungry, I'll just call room service later." *You and every other passenger on board.*

She almost asked Andy if he thought he might have eaten something bad but she didn't. She would have plenty of time to talk to him about that later. Right now, he needed to rest and get back on his feet.

Millie could fill in in a pinch but that was about it. No one could replace Andy, especially not her.

Millie told Andy she would check on him later in the day and headed to the door. She let herself out and slowly closed it behind her. She gave it a hard tug to make sure it had locked.

Instead of heading straight upstairs, she walked past the crew mess, which was empty, and then made a pit stop in the officer's dining room.

Millie pushed the tinted glass door open and stepped inside the dimly lit room. At first, Millie thought the room was empty, then she heard the murmur of soft voices that echoed from the dark corner.

Millie stepped further in.

Donovan and Veronica Chang sat together at a table in the corner. Their heads bent close together, almost touching.

They didn't notice Millie.

She cleared her throat. "Ahem."

Donovan's head shot up. "Hey Millie!"

"Hi Donovan." She nodded at Veronica who gave her a half-hearted smile. The young woman ran slender fingers through her jet-black hair and stared at Millie with her amber-colored cat eyes. Unblinking.

Her stare caused a shiver to run down Millie's spine. There was something about the woman...

"Are you looking for someone?" Donovan asked.

Millie shook her head. She had no idea why she had made the impulsive decision to stop in the private dining room.

"No one in particular," Millie answered vaguely. Before Donovan could ask another question Millie couldn't answer, she backed out of the room.

Why was Veronica talking to Donovan? Millie frowned. She hadn't seen the woman's application in the pile. She knew that the deadline had passed to apply for the job.

Was there something else? Another position that Veronica was trying to get?

She glanced down at the watch on her wrist. She had just enough time to make a quick stop in the theater to check on the staff before she headed up to the bridge to check on Scout.

The entire back of the stage blazed with bright lights, something Andy would have had a fit about, which was probably why they were on. Everyone knew Andy wouldn't be around.

Millie didn't mind the bright lights. There were times the backstage was downright creepy, especially at night when she was back there by herself.

She wandered over to Andy's chair and plopped down. His notebook was still on the table. Millie slipped on her glasses and flipped it open.

Andy kept meticulous notes of past schedules. She read the entries with interest. Andy had some great ideas for entertainment. She wondered why he had never implemented them.

Andy's pot of coffee sat on the table nearby. She lifted the container. It was half-empty.

Millie grabbed Andy's coffee cup, pulled it close and then poured some of the leftover coffee into the cup. She lifted it to her nose, about to take a sip when an odd odor wafted up. It was some sort of herb or chemical smell she couldn't put her finger on.

Millie dipped the tip of her finger in the brown liquid and lifted it to her lips. "Yuck!"

The coffee had a bitter taste and left a lingering metallic taste in her mouth. She wondered how Andy could have drank that much and not noticed the odd taste or weird smell.

Chapter 17

Footsteps echoed across the smooth stage floor.

Millie shoved the stopper in the top, grabbed the carafe and carried it to the dressing room. She needed to get the pot of coffee to the kitchen.

Several of the entertainment staff had stopped by to fill Millie in. Guests had started to trickle out into the common areas now that the ship had stopped bobbing around like a cork.

After the brief meeting, Millie had just enough time to make it up to the bridge to check on Scout and see if the captain wanted him out-and-about on the ship.

She knew she looked a little odd carrying a half-empty coffee pot around but she didn't dare leave it somewhere and chance someone emptying the contents.

Ingrid Kozlov answered the door when Millie knocked. Millie would be glad when she had her lanyard back and she could just let herself in.

The woman opened the door. Her eyes dropped to the carafe in Millie's hand. She grunted then walked back across the bridge, leaving Millie to trail behind her.

Captain Armati was front and center in the bridge. He briefly looked up and smiled when he saw Millie. "Good morning, Millie. I'm glad to see you haven't succumbed to the high seas."

She shrugged. "I guess I have a stronger stomach than I thought."

Captain turned to Ingrid. "I'll be right back."

He motioned Millie to follow him. They walked down the hall that led to the captain's apartment. Armati punched in the secret code and opened the door.

Millie followed him inside.

She spotted Scout, curled up on his bed next to the sliding glass doors. He opened his eyes but stayed put in his small bed.

Her heart lurched. Poor Scout didn't like the rough seas.

The captain bent down and stroked his head. "He's been like this all morning. Poor fella doesn't like the rocking and rolling."

Millie reached down and stroked his ears. He licked her finger, closed his eyes and sighed. She wasn't sure what one could give a dog for motion sickness. At least the seas had started to calm.

Captain stood. "I'm sure he'll back to his peppy self soon enough," he predicted.

Millie still had the carafe in her hand, which the captain had now noticed. "Do you always carry a pot of coffee around with you?" he joked.

Millie hesitated for a fraction of a second. "I think I'm holding a clue to Captain Vitale, the other crew and now Andy's mysterious illness."

He frowned. "I heard Andy was down in bed. I assumed it was the rough seas."

Millie shook her head. "Everyone, including Andy, told me he has never had motion sickness in all the years he's worked on the ships."

She lifted the carafe. "I found this in his office, sitting on his table. It's half empty. When I poured a small bit into his cup, I noticed an odd smell and when I tasted it..." She wrinkled her nose.

Captain reached for the carafe. "Let me try it." He took the carafe to the kitchen, set it on the counter and grabbed a coffee mug from inside the cabinet.

Millie had never seen the inside of the captain's kitchen, only a brief glimpse of the corner from the living room.

It was small but efficient. It had everything one would need to prepare a gourmet meal: standard size refrigerator, small electric stove with an oven and a microwave. It even had a dishwasher!

Armati lifted the stopper and poured a small amount of coffee in the cup. He lifted the cup and sniffed the contents. His brow furrowed. "It does have a faint odor, almost medicinal."

Next, he lifted the cup to his lips and took a small sip. He grimaced at the taste and wiped away the lingering residue with the back of his hand.

"Pretty bad, huh," Millie said.

Captain shook his head. "Andy drank this?"

"Yes. I think he did." Andy must have some hardy taste buds to stomach that stuff! "Maybe he mixed a lot of creamer and sugars and it disguised the taste."

Millie pointed at the pot. "I'm going to take this to the kitchen to see if Annette can tell me who delivered this to Andy. Someone on this ship is making the crew and staff sick."

Captain Armati nodded. "I heard you were reprimanded for sneaking into Donovan's office."

Millie's shoulders sank. "Yeah. It probably wasn't the brightest idea."

"Probably not," the captain agreed, "but I admire your loyalty to your friend."

Millie shoved the stopper in the top of the carafe and lifted it from the counter. "I hope Scout gets to feeling better."

Millie stopped on her way out to give him a little smooch on the head before she walked back into the bridge.

Captain Armati followed her out. She stopped at the door. "Would you like me to check on Scout later?"

Captain nodded. "I think he would like that."

A small smile lit Millie's face as she turned her back. Perhaps the captain would like it, too!

***

On her way to the kitchen, Millie swung by the gift shop to talk to Cat, who was behind the counter, hard at work. She caught Millie's eye as she rang up a purchase. She slipped the purchases into the bag and handed it to the customer.

Millie waited for the person to exit the store. "Been quiet around here?"

Cat shook her head. "No way!" She craned her neck and glanced at the shelves behind her – the ones that contained aspirin, cough drops, Band-Aids. One whole section of the shelf was empty.

"Let me guess. That was where the motion sickness medicine used to be," Millie said.

Cat snapped her fingers. "Bingo! I could have easily doubled the price and still sold out." She pointed at the coffee carafe in Millie's hand. "What'cha doing with that?"

Millie explained how Andy had fallen ill and that he was still down and out. She told Cat how she had found the carafe still sitting on his table. "You have anything I can put a little of this in so you can try it?"

Cat nodded. Her beehive hair-do bobbed up and down. "Yeah." Her head disappeared as she bent down and leaned into the cabinet. She popped back up, small plastic cup in her hand.

Millie poured a tiny amount of the brown liquid in the cup and held it out. "Smell this."

Cat stuck the cup under her nose and sniffed the contents. "Ugh!" She pushed the cup away and waved her hand under her nose. "That does not smell like coffee."

Millie thought it had a bit of a medicinal odor but it hadn't seemed that strong. Maybe Cat had a super-sensitive sniffer, which might be useful down the road. She filed that in the "might be useful" category of her brain. "Taste it."

Cat started to lift the cup to her lips.

"I would just dip the tip of your finger instead of drinking it," Millie advised.

"Good idea." Cat followed her suggestion and dipped her pinky in the cup. She licked the tip of her finger and frowned. "Yuck! What in the world?"

"I think someone poisoned Andy's coffee. It was probably the same person that poisoned Vitale and the other crew."

Cat slammed the cup on the counter. "I'd love to catch the thug in the act...or better yet, give them a dose of their own medicine."

Millie grinned. Cat had a wicked mind, but it did seem like a fitting punishment for the crime. Give them a taste of their own medicine. If they could only figure out who was behind it...

Chapter 18

Annette was nowhere in sight when Millie got to the kitchen. Amit was there, right next to the stove, chopping vegetables. "Hello, Miss Millie." He set the knife on the stainless steel counter and lifted the cutting board. He dumped the vegetables into a large, boiling pot before he turned back. "Miss Annette is on break."

"Okay. Thanks." Now was the perfect opportunity to talk to Amit about the poisonings. She was beginning to wonder if they were random – or if Captain Vitale, Andy and the other crew had been specific targets. She couldn't recall if Annette had even told her who the first victim had been.

Millie set the coffee carafe on the table. "Amit, do you remember the first person who became ill?"

Amit cocked his head thoughtfully. "It was Grace."

Grace was the dishwasher! Why would Grace be a target?

Millie looked beyond Amit, her eyes studying Grace, whose back was to Millie as she bent over the large, double sinks and rinsed dishes.

"What about Captain Vitale? You said you gave the lobster bisque to Suri and Suri said he got sidetracked and left it unattended in the warming bay."

"Yes, that's what he said."

"Did you see dish in the warming bay?"

Amit shook his head. "No. I don't recall. I was busy over in the bakery helping Noel."

Millie had almost forgotten about Noel...the same Noel who had applied for Annette's job. Millie wasn't even sure she was qualified for the position.

She turned her attention to Amit. Perhaps it was Amit, or even Suri.

Millie wanted to rule out Amit, she really did. She liked Amit and believed that he was loyal to Annette.

Grace stood upright as she reached for a dishtowel that hung on a hook nearby.

Millie stepped in beside the petite redhead. "Hi Grace. I think we met once before. I'm Millie, Assistant Cruise Director."

Grace dried her hands and replaced the towel. "Yes, I remember. You are friends with Miss Annette."

"Right."

Millie glanced behind her and lowered her voice. "Say, I know that you became ill not too long ago. Do you recall what you ate that may have caused you to become sick?"

Grace bit her lower lip. Her eyes dropped to the floor. "I-I…"

"You won't get in any trouble for telling me," Millie promised.

"Are you sure?" The girl was skittish. Millie wondered what was making her so nervous.

"Of course."

Grace looked over Millie's shoulder. "Follow me."

Millie followed her into the walk-in pantry, the one that Annette used to store all the dry goods like flour, sugar and coffee.

Grace shoved her hands in her apron pockets. "There was a small tray of lobster on the table near the exit door."

She peeked around Millie's shoulder to make sure they were still out of earshot. "The dish was ready to go. I had never tasted lobster before so I took one of the small dishes. No one would even miss it."

Raj, one of the dessert staff, wandered into the storeroom. He gave them an odd look before he grabbed a 10-lb. bag of flour and walked back out.

"And?" Millie prompted.

"It was about ten minutes later, my stomach started to churn, then I started to throw up. I couldn't stop."

"So you think it was the lobster?"

Grace nodded. "I thought there was something wrong with it so I dumped it in the trash. It was the only thing I had eaten all day."

"Did you tell Annette?"

Grace wrung her hands. "No. I told her I thought that maybe it was the tea. I didn't mention the lobster."

"Why not?"

"Because they are expensive and I wasn't supposed to eat them. They were headed to the captain's cabin for dinner."

Millie touched Grace's arm. "You're sure?"

"Yes." Grace nodded firmly. "All dishes headed to the captain's quarters have a special cover.

Instead of a brown cover, his are either silver or red."

Millie thanked her for sharing the information. She followed Grace out of the storage room, still holding the coffee pot. This was a huge clue. It meant that whoever poisoned the lobster had access to the kitchen.

Just like the lobster bisque and the coffee, that gave the individual opportunity. What about motive?

There was also a pattern. Whoever it was, was working their way down the ranks. Captain Armati was supposed to be first, and then second in command, Captain Vitale. Next would be Andy. Millie rubbed her brow. Who was in line after Andy?

Donovan was the next in line! On the other hand, maybe even Dave Patterson. Wouldn't that be something if someone tried to poison Patterson?

Millie had planned to take the coffee to Dave Patterson, Head of Security, but she made a pit stop at Donovan's office first.

She pushed open the half door that separated the lobby from the employee area and rounded the corner.

She stood outside Donovan's door and knocked.

"Come in," a muffled voice called from the other side.

Millie grabbed the door handle, twisted down and pushed it open.

Donovan was inside and alone. He leaned back in the chair when he saw Millie. "How kind of you to bring me coffee," he said.

The smile disappeared. "How's Andy?"

Millie pulled out a chair and plopped down. "On the mend. He's still in bed but his color is a bit better."

Donovan nodded. "Good. I'm glad to hear it."

He folded his hands behind his head and leaned back in his chair. "So what brings you here?"

"This!" She set the carafe on the desktop and slid it toward him. "Taste it."

Donovan leaned forward and reached for the handle. "Where did you get this?"

"Andy's office. It was there this morning. He drank this right before he became ill," she explained.

Donovan opened his top desk drawer and pulled out a mug. By now, the coffee had to be downright cold. He pulled the stopper and poured a small bit in his mug.

Donovan lifted it to his lips.

"I would smell it first and don't take a big sip," she warned.

Donovan eyed her over the rim of the cup and nodded.

He sniffed the contents. "It has a bit of an odor."

"Like Nyquil?" she suggested.

"Yeah, kind of like that." He tasted the liquid then lowered the cup. "Not too bad but a bit of a bitter taste."

"Right."

Donovan set the mug on the desk. He lifted his gaze and studied Millie. He knew her well enough to know the wheels were spinning in her head. She had a theory, of that he was certain.

"What are your thoughts?"

"I'm glad you asked. I think that someone is trying to sabotage Annette and they're doing it by poisoning the ship's officers."

"How so? The first person that became ill was a kitchen crew. Grace something…"

"Right," Millie agreed. "I just talked to Grace. She was poisoned from sampling a plate of lobster from a tray that was on its way to Captain Armati's apartment."

Donovan lifted a brow. "Really? Why is it that we just discovered this now?"

"Because Grace is terrified she'll be fired for stealing."

"Stealing a bite of food?" Donovan had never known a crewmember who had been fired over a missing dish.

Now someone breaking into his office in the middle of the night? That was a different story!

Millie explained how after Grace ate the dish, she thought maybe there was something wrong with it and had tossed the rest of the lobster in the trash but didn't dare tell anyone. She had blamed it on the tea instead.

"Captain Vitale was number two when he was poisoned by the lobster bisque. Today it was Andy."

Millie dropped the bomb. "I think you're next!"

Chapter 19

"Me?"

Millie scooted her chair close to the desk. "Yes. It will be either you or Dave Patterson."

Donovan replaced the stopper and pushed the container across the desk. "What do you suggest we do?"

Millie rubbed her temples. "I'm not sure yet. I just made the connection."

She jumped out of the chair and reached for the carafe. "Let me get back to you. I'm on my way to see Patterson now."

Millie turned on her heel and headed to the door. The carafe was lighter now. She was running out of samples. She hoped she would have enough left to give Patterson a taste.

"Millie!" Donovan stopped her at the door.

She spun back around. "Hmm?"

"You're a sweetheart. I don't care what anyone else says!" He winked.

"But…" She realized he was teasing her. "Same here." She grabbed the door handle and stepped outside.

***

Millie had one more stop before it was time to get back to work. She needed to be on hand in case the staff needed help, although the majority of them probably knew more than she did!

Millie passed Annette on her way down to Deck 2 where Dave Patterson's office was located.

She looked frazzled. "Whew! What a day!"

Millie nodded. "I was looking for you earlier. Amit said you had taken a break."

"Yeah, my first break of the day. I'm headed back to the kitchen now." Annette pointed to the coffee pot. "What's that for?"

Millie held it up. "It'll take too long to explain but I think I finally got a break in the case."

Annette pressed her hands to her flushed cheeks. "That would be a miracle."

"I'll stop by after I'm off duty later tonight." Millie wasn't certain what time that would be, not with Andy out of commission and the entire entertainment schedule resting squarely on her shoulders. She patted the walkie-talkie on her hip. "I'll radio you later."

Millie picked up the pace as she turned the corner and headed down the long corridor in the direction of Patterson's office.

When she reached the door, she could see dim light through the frosted glass pane.

Millie tapped lightly. There was no answer so Millie turned the knob and pushed the door open.

Patterson was talking on the phone. He held up a finger and continued his conversation. "I don't care if the passenger is threating to sue. If he doesn't calm down, you need to throw him in the hoosegow 'til he sobers up."

Patterson set the receiver in the cradle and grimaced. "The natives are getting restless," he joked.

Millie set the coffee carafe on the desk and pulled out a chair. "I would imagine on top of feeling seasick, they're starting to get cabin fever."

"Yep." Patterson changed the subject. "What brings you to my neck of the woods?"

Millie pointed to the pot. "This and the string of poisonings. You heard about Andy?"

Patterson nodded. "His could be a case of seasickness."

Millie shook her head. "Everyone, including Andy himself, said he has never experienced motion sickness."

Millie went on. "I think he was poisoned by the contents of this carafe."

Dave Patterson slid the pot across the table. He pulled the stopper and lifted it to his nose. "Coffee?" he asked.

"Yeah. Do you smell the odd odor?"

"I do. He reached in his drawer and pulled out a small vial. He poured a sample into the container and then screwed the lid on.

"Aren't you going to taste it?" Millie asked. "I mean, what if I'm wrong?"

Patterson swiped his index finger across the lip of the carafe and wiped it on his tongue. He turned his gaze to Millie. "You may be onto something."

Millie repeated everything she had told Donovan – about Grace and the lobster dish, the lobster bisque left unattended and then mysteriously materializing in the officer's dining room.   Last but not least, she told him how she'd found the carafe in Andy's office.

"Whoever is doing this is working their way down the list." Millie held out an index finger. "First, Grace, but that dish was intended for Captain Armati." She held up a second finger. "Second, Captain Vitale and the lobster bisque. Next in line was Andy."

Patterson leaned back in his chair and fixed his searing blue eyes on Millie, who immediately began to sweat: her forehead, her armpits, the crease behind her knee...

She forced her eyes to glaze over. That was the only way she could concentrate. "I think next in line is either you or Donovan."

Patterson thumbed his chest. "Me?"

Millie nodded. "Yep. The two of you are next in command."

Patterson drummed his fingers on the desk. "We need to set up a trap to catch them in the act."

Millie nodded. She liked where his train of thought was going. "We need to act fast before they make their next move."

Patterson watched Millie as she strolled out of his office and down the long corridor. She could feel his eyes bore into the back of her head.

She wondered why he always made her so nervous. Maybe it was because it seemed he was trying to mess with her head or figure out what made her tick, which should be easy.

There wasn't much to Millie Sanders. What you see is what you get.

Chapter 20

Millie went right from Patterson's office to her new command post – Andy's office. A small army of staff had gathered around the table.

Zack jumped up when he saw Millie. He motioned her to Andy's seat. She squeezed in at the table. "How are we doing?"

"So far, so good," Alison told her. "There's a bit more passenger interaction now that the seas aren't as rough."

"Which means I think we'll have a full house for tonight's headliner," Kevin piped up.

Millie nodded. Tonight's show was the Broadway musical, *Grease*. It was new to the crew and the performers had only run through it the last couple of weeks.

"Is there anything I need to worry about or take care of?" Millie asked.

The group shook their heads. It was all under control as far as they knew. It was almost running too smoothly, which scared Millie. Nothing ever went that smooth, at least not for her.

After the meeting ended, she checked in with the sound crew and the lighting crew. She also stopped by the makeup area and dressing room.

Although she trusted the staff to keep her apprised of problems, Millie decided to walk the ship from top to bottom.

She started at the sky deck, which was empty, before she made a pit stop in the VIP area.

A couple of guests lounged in the chairs and Millie smiled as she made a pass through.

Next was the chapel, followed by the spa and fitness center. Her eyes fell on the boxing ring. It seemed eons ago that she had been inside the ring, waiting for Andy to zap her.

Millie wandered down the steps and onto the lido deck. The sun split through the clouds. Millie turned her face to the warmth and closed her eyes for a moment. The sun was a welcome sight.

She opened her eyes and glanced down at the seas. The waters had calmed. Perhaps they would be able to stop at South Seas Cay, after all.

The deck chairs around the pool had started to fill and the band had set up. The relaxing rhythm of Caribbean steel drums filled the air.

Millie methodically checked each public area deck by deck. She finished her tour on Deck 2, outside the medical center.

She stopped by the crew mess and fixed a plate of food then took it back to her cabin. It would be nice to have a few moments of peace and quiet so she could focus on the investigation.

Millie pulled out her handy-dandy pad of paper and pen to work on her list of suspects. At the top of the list, she wrote Amit's name. Next, she put Noel, then Suri. She tapped her pen on the pad of paper. Veronica Chang still lingered in the back of her mind. There was something about that woman.

Still, she didn't have a motive. Millie remembered seeing Donovan and Veronica in the corner of the officer's dining room. Millie jotted her name at the bottom of the list.

She made a mental note to ask Annette about her. Veronica worked under Annette, which meant she had opportunity but lacked motive.

If Captain Armati stopped in South Seas Cay the next day, Millie wouldn't have time to work on the case. She would have shore duty, and that meant she would be leaving on the first shuttle in the morning, returning on the last shuttle back to the ship later in the day.

Millie finished her fish, picked at the tasteless mashed potatoes and ate two bites of crusty bread. Her stomach was still a bit queasy and she didn't want to risk getting ill. No way could both Andy and she be out of commission at the same time.

Millie dropped her dirty dishes in the cafeteria and stopped outside Andy's door. She tapped softly.

"It's unlocked."

Millie turned the handle and stepped into Andy's cabin. He was sitting on the couch, watching TV. He still looked a bit under the weather but the color had returned to his face and he smiled when he saw Millie.

Andy muted the TV. "I heard you're doing an excellent job," he told her.

Millie turned a hint of pink. "I'm trying hard," she confessed. "I've had a lot of help from the awesome staff and crew. Everyone has chipped in to help. I couldn't do it without them."

She went on. "You look much better."

Andy ran a hand through his spiked red hair. "I feel a lot better, like I might actually live to see another day."

"Speaking of that," Millie sat on the edge of the sofa, opposite Andy, "there was a coffee carafe on your table earlier. Was it yours?"

Andy nodded. "I drink a pot every morning. Like clockwork."

"Do you remember who brought it to you?"

Andy shifted on the couch. He frowned. "No, but now that you ask, it was odd. Usually someone from the kitchen drops it off, but for some reason it was already on the table when I got there this morning."

"Do you remember an odd taste or smell?"

Andy rubbed the stubble on his chin. "Yeah, it tasted a tad bitter so I added some extra sugar. After that it was fine."

It dawned on him where Millie was going with her questions. "You think someone poisoned me?"

She nodded. "Patterson took a sample from the pot and is sending it in for testing."

"But who would want to poison me?"

"The same person that poisoned Captain Vitale!"

Millie spent the rest of the evening bouncing back and forth from theater to lounges to bars to the lido deck. The buzz of the ship was back to normal and the seas were calm.

After the main show ended, the theater cleared. Millie waited outside the dressing room for the performers to change out of their costumes.

One-by-one, the staff filtered out and one-by-one, Millie thanked them for everything they had done that day.

When Zack came out, Millie repeated the words. "Zack, I don't know what I would've done without your help today. I want you to know that I appreciate it more than words can express."

Zack leaned forward and wrapped Millie in a bear hug. "And we don't know what we would do without you. You're the glue that holds us together."

Tears stung the back of Millie's eyes at the unexpected praise. She was just doing her job. A job that she loved...a job that made her feel needed, important, and special. On top of that, she worked with a crew that felt like family – her family.

Zack kissed her cheek, winked and darted off the stage.

The last one out of the room was Alison. She hugged Millie, too. "Shall we?" She made a sweeping motion off the stage.

Millie shut off the lights and closed the dressing room door.

The women wandered across the stage and down the steps. Alison reached for the rail. "I heard a rumor that there may have been something in Andy's coffee that made him sick."

Millie nodded. "It's starting to look that way."

Alison followed Millie down the side steps and then fell in line as they walked side-by-side out of the theater. "I know who dropped the coffee off this morning. I caught a glimpse of them as I made my way to the dressing room."

***

Millie stopped dead in her tracks. "Wh-who was it?" Her heart began to pound. Alison may very well be able to crack the case!

The tall blonde frowned. "Well, I'm not sure on the name. You know, I don't hang out around the kitchen too much." She brightened. "I think I could identify them if I saw them again."

Alison went on to give a brief description of the suspect. "Although, it was dark and I didn't get a close look at the face." Millie wasn't sure if the description of the suspect was a surprise or not.

It was late. The kitchen ran on a skeleton crew until 11:30 and then only room service staff worked the late shift.

The main kitchen had already closed. They would have to wait until the next morning.

"Can you meet me in front of the casino tomorrow morning at say, 8:00 a.m.?" That would give Alison and Millie enough time to scope out the kitchen before they had to report to work.

Alison nodded. "Of course."

Millie and Alison parted ways when Millie stopped in front of her cabin door and Alison continued down the hall.

Millie stood and watched Alison's blonde hair swing back and forth. She looked like an angel. A beautiful, blonde angel had come to save the day.

Chapter 21

Millie tossed and turned all night. She hoped that they would be able to catch the culprit before a fourth victim succumbed.

She crawled out of bed before the alarm sounded. Her feet hit the floor and she padded quietly across the carpet, slipped inside the bathroom and flipped on the light.

Millie leaned in and studied her reflection in the mirror...not bad for six decades. She turned to the left and studied the side of her face then tugged on several hair strands.

It was time for a haircut...not too much though. She still preferred to pull it back and away from her face. Maybe chop just enough off so that if she wanted to wear it down, it didn't look like a tangled mop on top of her head.

Millie showered and dressed in record time.

Sarah stirred in her bunk as Millie slipped on her shoes and grabbed her radio and lanyard.

She tiptoed out of the cabin and quietly closed the door.

She glanced to the left, in the direction of the crew mess before she decided to head topside to the buffet area to check on the seas and to see how far the ship had traveled overnight.

The last she had heard was that the captain was leaning towards steaming on to Jamaica and hitting the private island on the way back to Miami.

Millie walked along the rail and stared out at the water. She was getting good at judging the waves and although they weren't nearly as tall as they had been the day before, they were still strong. Shuttle boats would be out of the question.

The buffet area was packed. Millie grabbed a plate, and placed a few slices of bacon, some dry toast and a box of corn flakes cereal on top. She didn't have the patience to wait in the long lines for hot food. Not today.

Millie smiled and nodded to a few of the passengers as she walked the aisle and headed outdoors. Everyone had the same idea in mind and the outside bistro tables were full.

There was a small section, one deck up, with a cluster of chairs most guests never even noticed.

Millie climbed the stairs and plopped into a corner chair that faced the open water. She balanced her plate on her lap and bowed her head in prayer, thanking the Lord for calm seas and asking for help in solving the mystery.

After Millie finished her food, she carried her dirty dishes down the steps and dropped them in the bin. She had just enough time to stop by Andy's office before she rendezvoused with Alison in front of the casino.

She breathed a sigh of relief at her first glimpse of light beaming out from the back of the stage. Andy was in his normal spot, his head bent over his big, black book.

He looked up when he heard Millie approach. A smile beamed across his face. "You're up bright and early."

"So are you," she pointed out. She pulled out the chair next to Andy and flopped down. "You look great."

"You don't look so bad yourself," he teased.

Andy tapped his pen on top of the open notebook. "I heard yesterday went off without a hitch, thanks to you."

Millie refused to take all of the credit. "No, not just me, thanks to all of the staff and crew that pitched in and made my job easy. You would have been proud."

Andy nodded. "I am. In fact, I'm planning a surprise for you, for all of you as a token of my appreciation."

He went on. "But not for today. Today is another sea day and from past experience, the natives will be restless."

Andy pointed at his carafe of coffee and cringed. "I haven't tried it yet. I'm almost afraid to drink it."

Millie pulled the coffee close and lifted the stopper. She sniffed the top. It smelled like coffee, with nary a trace of a medicinal odor. "Would you like me to try it first?" she offered.

Andy shook his head. "No. I think it will be okay."

She glanced at her watch and sprung to her feet. "I think we may be hot on the heels of the culprit. Alison caught a glimpse of the person who dropped off the carafe yesterday morning."

Andy raised a brow. "Really? Who was it?"

"She doesn't know the name." Millie shrugged her shoulders. "I'm meeting her in a few minutes near the galley so she can go inside and hopefully positively ID the person."

She slid the chair under the table. "I'll be back." Millie turned on her heel and power-walked across the back stage and out of the theater.

Alison was already waiting at the casino entrance when Millie arrived. "Ready?"

Alison nodded. "Yep."

Millie opened the side door that led into the kitchen. Alison followed behind. The galley was buzzing with activity as staff darted here and there.

The girls snaked back and forth across the kitchen.

Alison studied the kitchen crew with a sharp eye. She leaned close to Millie and pointed. "I think that's her!"

Millie followed her gaze. It was Noel Kalani!

Millie needed to corner Annette, tell her what she knew so she could keep an eye on Noel.

"You've been a huge help, Alison. Thank you."

The girls wove their way out of the kitchen, around the gleaming counters and rows of cabinets as they headed to the revolving doors that connected the kitchen to the main dining room.

The girls stood off to the side and waited as several crewmembers hustled through the door.

Alison grabbed Millie's arm and tugged. "Wait! I-I think it might have been her instead!" She nodded her head at Veronica Chang, who had just walked by.

Millie's heart sunk. Now they had two people to watch: Noel Kalani and Veronica Chang!

The girls wandered back to the theater.

Andy and Millie finished the schedule. She was relieved things were back to normal, whatever "normal" was.

The morning flew by as Millie darted from activity to activity. Everything ran like clockwork.

On her first break, Millie headed to the bridge. Ingrid, in her usual surly mood, opened the door to let Millie enter, and then stalked off.

The captain was nowhere in sight as Millie wandered across the bridge and to the captain's private quarters. She wondered when Captain Vitale would return and she hoped he was feeling better now.

Millie tapped on the door and waited. No one answered. Millie punched in the secret code, which the captain had given her some time ago, and let herself into the apartment.

Scout met her at the door. His whole body quivered as he waited for Millie to pick him up. He squirmed and wiggled as she held him close. He licked the end of her nose, her chin and then grabbed a chunk of hair that had somehow managed to escape her messy bun.

After a quick trip outside, Millie grabbed his leash and carrier next to the door and the two headed out. She still had enough time to talk to Annette – if she hurried.

Millie placed Scout inside his carrier, shifted the carrier to her shoulder and stepped into the large kitchen.

Annette was up to her elbows in some sort of dough. When she saw Millie, she wiped her hands on her apron and waved her to the dry goods storage. "I heard you were in here earlier with one of the dancers."

Millie nodded. "Yep. Alison saw the person who dropped off Andy's carafe yesterday morning."

Annette's eyes widened. "And?"

"It's good and bad news," Millie admitted.

"Start with the good."

"She was able to positively ID the suspects."

"So what's the bad?" Annette asked.

"Suspects. It could be one of two people: Noel Kalani or Veronica Chang. She only got a brief glimpse of the side of the face and backside as they walked away. Plus it was dark."

Annette rolled her eyes. "So now what?"

"I've given it some thought. Next in line is either Donovan Sweeney or Dave Patterson." Millie went on. "Think about it. Whoever it is, is working their way down the ranks. Captain Armati was 'supposed' to be first. Next was Captain Vitale, then Andy."

"The next in rank would be either Donovan or Patterson, although I'm leaning towards Donovan. Who in their right mind would try to poison the head of security?" Other than a mentally unstable person - maybe it wasn't that far off, after all...

Annette tapped her foot on the floor. "So we need to catch them in the act."

"Annette!" A frantic voice echoed from the galley.

"Look, I gotta run but we need to give this some thought. If we put our heads together, I'm sure we can come up with something."

Millie agreed. "The sooner, the better. I think one of them is going to make a move. If not today, tomorrow."

Millie headed out of the kitchen and to the gift shop to talk to Cat.

Maribelle, who had transferred from dining room staff and recently started working in the gift shop, was on duty.

Millie and Scout headed to the back. The place was brimming with shoppers.

Maribelle looked a bit stressed out as she pushed a strand of hair from her eyes. She leaned over to peek inside the carrier. "Hey buddy."

"Scout," Millie told her.

"Scout," Maribelle repeated. "Aren't you just the most adorable fella?"

Scout licked her thumb. "Ruff!"

She stood upright. "Cat doesn't come in for another hour." Maribelle groaned as she studied the hordes of shoppers. "Not soon enough, in my opinion."

"Well, you look like you have it all under control," Millie assured her. She gave Maribelle a smile of encouragement and squeezed her arm before she zigzagged around the throngs of shoppers to the safety of the hall corridor.

Confined spaces and crowds of people caused Millie to feel a bit on the claustrophobic side.

She stopped by Cat's cabin and knocked. No one answered.

Millie knew there were only a couple places Cat could be, other than her cabin, and one of those was the crew mess.

Scout and Millie stepped inside. Her eyes scanned the room. She caught a glimpse of Cat over in the corner. She was seated at a table with two other women Millie didn't recognize.

Millie grabbed a glass of water and shuffled over to the table. "Mind if I have a seat?"

Cat waved her in. "No, of course not." She pointed to the woman on her left. "This is Maria." She pointed to the other woman. "This is Novi."

Millie smiled and pulled out the chair. She set Scout and his carrier on the floor next to her chair. "I'm Millie." She shook hands with each of them.

The girls chit chatted for a few moments. Not long after, Maria and Novi left.

Cat picked up the pickle spear on the edge of her plate. "So what's going on?" She eyed Millie with interest.

Millie explained what she had discovered up to that point.

Cat nibbled the end of the pickle thoughtfully. "We need a plan."

"Pronto," Millie agreed. "I think I have an idea."

Chapter 22

After Millie had finished laying out her plan, Cat leaned back in her chair and crossed her arms. "I think that will work but how do you think Annette will react when she finds out she's not a part of our covert operation?"

Millie knew her friend would not like it, not one bit, but first of all, she was too close to the case and second of all, it would be too obvious for her to be directly involved.

The girls headed upstairs and parted ways outside the gift shop. Cat made her way inside the crowded store while Millie and Scout headed to the kitchen.

The place had cleared out, the lunch rush over. Annette was over near the spice cabinet, poking around inside.

"There you are," Millie said to the back of her head.

Annette swung around and faced Millie. She was wearing a pair of dark sunglasses.

"What in the world?"

"My cornucopias are bothering me," Annette said in a loud voice. Not that anyone was paying attention. The room was almost empty. "The glaring lights...I can hardly see."

"Your cornucopia..." Annette had officially lost it.

"You mean corneas?" Millie asked.

Annette waved a hand dismissively. "Yeah, that!"

Millie glanced at the clock. "I need to make a few rounds. Will you be here for a bit?"

Annette nodded. The sunglasses slipped on her nose and she promptly pushed them back into place. "Yep."

Millie made a quick pit stop in the buffet area where she grabbed a turkey sandwich on a pretzel roll and an extra slice of turkey for Scout.

They wandered up to their small oasis on the other side of the mini golf course.

Millie placed Scout's carrier on the deck and unzipped the sides.

Scout hopped out of the carrier and made a beeline for his potty pad. After he finished his business, he stopped for a dip in his pool, which Millie had quickly filled with water.

Millie placed bits of turkey on a paper napkin and he nibbled on the goodies while she enjoyed her own lunch.

Several guests stopped to visit and admire their new hangout. Millie loved the new spot. It was perfect for escaping the crowds.

After they finished eating, Millie picked up one of the balls and tossed it to the other side of the enclosure.

Scout misjudged the speed of the ball as he got hung up on top of it and the ball rolled him over.

Finally, he tired of the game and sprawled out under Millie's lounge chair for an afternoon siesta.

Millie let him nap for a few minutes, until her break was over. She felt bad that she had to wake him up, but even the short time he slept gave him his second wind and he pranced around her feet as she gathered the dirty dishes.

Millie snapped his leash to his small collar and the two of them headed across the deck. The sunshine warmed her shoulders as they strolled along. The pool decks and bar areas were at full capacity as guests enjoyed the warm, tropical weather.

She spent the next hour hosting trivia outside the casino. It was all about chocolate, one of Millie's favorite foods!

Trivia ended and Millie headed to guest services for her next assignment, which was to find out how many complaints they had received over the revised schedule of activities Millie had managed to throw together the day before.

Nikki, Sarah's friend, was nowhere in sight. Instead, a young man Millie had never seen before stepped up to the counter. His hazel colored eyes peered at her over the top of his thick black glasses. "Yes?"

Millie lifted Scout and tucked him in the crook of her arm. When the young man spied Scout, he wrinkled his nose. "I heard there was a dog on board. What an ugly mutt," he sneered.

Millie could feel her ears warm and her blood began to boil. She opened her mouth to say something smart and thought better of it. Instead, she tightened her jaw. "Yes, I'm Millie Sanders, Assistant Cruise Director."

The man glanced at her nametag. "Okay."

"I'm here to see if guests have lodged any complaints," she added stiffly.

"Let me check." He turned on his heel and stepped over to the side where a couple other guest services staff were milling about.

After a brief conversation, he returned. "The only complaint we've heard so far is that we ran out of barf bags."

"Thank you." She turned to go.

"Of course, the day is young. I'm sure if you stop back by later, we'll have at least a couple," he said nastily.

This turd was really testing her patience. She spun back around. Her eyes narrowed and she leaned over the counter. "What is your name?" she asked in a clipped voice.

Mr. Personality reached up and grabbed his nametag. He tugged on his shirt so Millie had a close up shot of his name. "Zane. Zane Gretski," he said. "My father is Vice President of Sales at the Miami office."

Millie couldn't help herself. This young man was pushing all her buttons. "Congratulations."

She stiffened her back and she and Scout marched across the lobby and up the stairs. She made a mental note to avoid Zane Gretski from here on out. If not, her mouth would surely get her in hot water!

The rest of the afternoon flew by. Scout and she checked in on several of the activities. The schedule was sailing as smooth as the seas.

As she worked, she finished formulating her plan to catch the culprit in the act. Now, if only she could get Annette on board!

By the time her next break rolled around, dinner was over and it was time for Scout to return home. His brisk trot had slowed to a stroll. It had been a full day and all of the activities had taken their toll.

The door that led to the bridge was ajar. Millie and Scout slipped inside and Millie quietly closed the door behind them. Captain Armati was off to one side, talking on the phone when she stepped inside the bridge. She waited until he finished his conversation then walked across the room.

"Is there any news on Captain Vitale?"

Armati's expression was grim. "I just found out we almost lost him." He sucked in a deep breath and straightened his shoulders. "But he's getting better by the day. Judging by his insistence that he return to the ship before we get back to Miami, I'd say he's almost 100% recovered."

Armati had a question of his own. "How is your investigation going?"

"Good," she answered. "I have it narrowed down to two suspects." Even if Millie told him the names, she doubted he would recognize them without seeing their faces. "Both of them work in the kitchen with Annette."

She snuggled Scout one last time and handed him over to Captain Armati. "We had a great day. He's pooped and we both love Ocean Oasis."

Ocean Oasis was the nickname Millie had given their cozy little retreat.

Armati's face beamed. "I'm glad to hear that." He balanced Scout with one hand and reached for his carrier. "Are you going ashore in Jamaica tomorrow?"

Millie frowned. She hadn't thought that far ahead. The last time she and Annette had gotten off on the island, it had been scary.

She had heard horror stories of unsuspecting guests and crew robbed at gunpoint, not far from the port. "I don't know."

"If you don't have plans, perhaps I can entice you to join me for a couple hours on shore. Dunn River Falls is spectacular and not far from the falls is a great little spot to have a bite to eat."

Millie's mouth turned Sahara Desert. He was inviting her on a date!

She must have had the deer-in-the-headlights look on her face.

"Unless, of course, you don't want to go."

"N-no. That sounds lovely. What time?" she asked. No way did she want Captain Armati to think she was turning him down!

She would have to wait until the first wave of passengers had disembarked since Andy and she had to see them off near the gangway.

"How does eleven sound?"

Millie nodded. "Great. What should I wear?"

"A bathing suit, shorts and probably a t-shirt will work," he told her.

"Bring a pair of water shoes," he added, "wet rocks get slippery."

Millie had never climbed waterfalls before. She had seen plenty of them in her lifetime. The Upper Peninsula of Michigan had quite a few.

They agreed to meet near the exit at 11:00 on the dot.

Millie made her way out of the bridge and into the hall. Her heart skipped a beat. She – Millie Sanders – had an honest-to-goodness date!

Chapter 23

Millie had a couple hours to kill before the kitchen cleared out and she could talk to Annette. She stopped by the headliner show. Tonight was the illusionist. She watched for several long moments while a young woman on stage disappeared then reappeared.

Andy was behind the curtain, peeking out at the performance when Millie got there. He turned as she approached. "Did you stop by guest services?"

She nodded. "Yes. They have a young man that works back there and he's a total..."

Andy finished the sentence. "...jerk by the name of Zane Gretski."

"So you've met him too."

Andy nodded. "Unfortunately, and unfortunately, we're stuck with him until who knows when. Although I predict it will not be much longer. Rumor has it he has managed to work his way through four different ships in the last year. Let's just say that he wears out his welcome rather quickly."

Millie grimaced. "Why in the world would they put someone like that in guest services?"

Andy lifted his head and raised a brow. "Because *Mister* Gretski thinks he's too good to work in the kitchen or cleaning departments."

He changed the subject. "Any complaints?"

Millie shook her head. "No. Not unless you count running out of barf bags."

Millie lowered her voice and imitated Zane's annoying nasal voice. "But come back later. I'm sure we'll have something by then."

"Not bad." Andy chuckled. "How is the investigation going?"

Millie told him what they had so far and that she had it narrowed down to Veronica Chang and Noel Kalani.

"Do I have tomorrow off?" she suddenly asked, remembering the captain's invitation.

The illusionist ended his show.

Andy pulled the curtain to the side. "Be right back. Wait here."

Millie watched as Andy took front and center stage, and wrapped up the show. He thanked the passengers for their patience during the storm and apologized for any discomfort they had experienced.

The lights went up and the theater began to clear out.

Andy stepped back behind the stage and picked up the conversation where they left off. "Yes. You have part of tomorrow off. After the first wave of passengers disembark until they start to return." It would give Millie about five hours of free time.

"Great," Millie said.

Andy's eyes narrowed. Millie was up to something. "Going somewhere special?" he fished.

"Maybe." She averted her gaze and stared at the floor.

She might as well spill the beans. There was no way the captain and she could sneak off the ship. Someone or probably lots of someones, would see them disembark together and tongues would wag, for sure.

"Captain Armati invited me to visit Dunn River Falls tomorrow," she admitted.

Andy lifted a brow and nodded. Andy had never seen the captain show an interest in any of the staff. He had heard the story how the captain's wife had died while he was at sea. He had also heard that Captain Armati had dinner with Millie in his apartment not long ago.

Andy wasn't one for gossip. There were plenty enough crew on board to take care of that. "Have a nice afternoon off," is all that he said.

The theater had cleared. The entertainment staff had disappeared. Only Andy and Millie remained.

Andy flicked the panel of lights to the "off" position and the two of them wandered down the long hall and out of the theater.

"Could you take a run by Paradise Lounge to check on karaoke?"

She nodded. "Of course." He had never asked her to go there. She had always checked in at the Tahitian Nights Dance Club. Maybe he was trying to switch things up.

Millie made her way to the club. The place was packed! A woman on the stage was belting out a sultry blues song. The crowd sang along.

Satisfied everything was as it should be, she stepped into the atrium area where soft piano music floated in the air.

Millie's stomach growled. She couldn't remember the last time she'd eaten. Now that she thought about it, it had been up at Ocean Oasis with Scout!

She slid into the pizza station and grabbed a slice of pepperoni before heading to the open deck. Stray strands of hair danced across her face as a cool ocean breeze lifted them. She tucked the strands behind her ear and nibbled the tip of her pizza.

Off in the distance, Millie thought she caught a twinkle of lights. The ship had slowed as it glided through the dark, still waters.

Her gaze lowered from the lights to the ship's wake. It had been a long few days. Millie felt the tension leave her body and her shoulders relaxed.

Tomorrow would be both exciting and terrifying. Exciting to spend part of her day with Captain Armati, exploring an island she knew little about, other than the short time she and Annette had spent trying to track down Olivia LaShay's killer.

What little she could remember was of a lush, tropical jungle island. It reminded her of the other islands they visited. It would be fun to explore and discover something new.

She finished the best part of the pizza, leaving the crust on the plate and reluctantly stepped away from the railing.

It was time to work out the details of the sting and clear Annette's name!

***

Millie reached Deck 7 and Cat's gift shop just as it was closing. Her timing was perfect. Cat had just locked the door.

Millie leaned her hip against the plate glass window. "Are you ready for this?"

Cat nodded. Her beehive was slightly off kilter and she lifted her hands to straighten it. Millie remembered Cat's story of how her abusive ex-husband had grabbed a handful of her hair when she tried to escape and then stabbed her.

She wondered if Cat kept it up as a way to protect herself. If she kept her hair up and out of reach, no one could ever grab it again.

Then she wondered if Cat took it down every night before she went to bed. The thought of birds building a nest in her hair flickered through her mind. She smiled.

"What's so funny?" Cat asked.

The smiled faded. "Oh nothing." She didn't dare speak her thoughts and chance hurting Cat's feelings.

Annette was pacing the floor when the girls stepped into the kitchen. She was still wearing the sunglasses. "It's about time! I almost gave up on you two," she grumbled.

Cat pointed to the dark shades. "What's up with the sunglasses?"

"Her corneas are burning," Millie explained.

Annette whipped the sunglasses off and handed them to Cat. "That was just an excuse.

These aren't really sunglasses, they're *spy glasses*. Here, try them on."

Cat slid them on and turned to Millie. "Wow, there isn't much of a tint."

"Watch this." Annette deftly sidestepped Cat and stood behind her. She waved her hand.

Cat lifted her arm, snaked it around behind her and grabbed Annette's hand. "Hey! I can see you!"

"Exactly. The inside of the glasses are a mirror. It's like having eyes in the back of my head!"

Milly finally caught on. "So you're spying on people - watching your own back so-to-speak."

Annette snapped her fingers. "Bingo!"

Cat handed them to Millie. She slid them on and slowly walked around the room. It was fun to see what was going on behind her but also distracting. She wasn't watching where she was

271

going and ran into the corner of the cabinet. "Ouch!"

Millie took them off and handed them back.

"Gotta be careful." Annette slipped them into her front shirt pocket. "So what's the plan?"

She laid out her theory that the culprit was going in order of rank and ended with. "I think either Dave Patterson or Donovan Sweeney is next on the list. We need to set up a sting, arrange it so Cat and I can trail the two suspects, Noel and Veronica, and catch one of them in the act."

"What about me?" Annette asked.

"You're too close to the investigation. You need to stay here to make sure we didn't miss anything," Millie explained.

The answer seemed to pacify Annette. She shoved her hands behind her back and started to pace. "What if I make a really big deal of making a special dish for the officers? I go on and on about how I'm trying to prove that my food is safe."

Millie picked up. "So you plate them up, labeling the individual dishes with each of the officer's names."

Cat caught on. "We make sure that Veronica and Noel take Donovan and Patterson's dishes…"

Annette snapped her fingers. "Voila! We have our poisonaire!"

Cat frowned. "Poisonaire?"

"I just made that up," Annette admitted.

She went on. "We'll have to make sure everyone is back on board for this to work. How does a happy hour dish sound?"

Millie could tip off Donovan and Patterson to their plan tomorrow morning before she got off the ship. "Perfect. I'll be back on board in plenty of time. What time should Cat and I get here?"

Two sets of eyes swung around and stared at Millie quizzically. "Where are you going tomorrow?" Annette was surprised. Millie hadn't seemed at all interested in Jamaica...

Millie dropped her gaze to the gleaming counter top and wiped at an imaginary spot with the tip of her finger. "Oh, to Dunn River Falls and maybe lunch."

Cat propped her elbows on the table and dropped her chin in her hand. "Alone?" she probed.

"No."

"Patterson?" Annette guessed.

Millie rolled her eyes. "No, not Patterson. Captain Armati."

Cat sucked in a breath. "My, my," she clucked.

Annette slapped an open palm on the counter. "I knew it! I knew he had the hots for you!"

Millie's face reddened. "Captain Armati does not have the hots for me!" she protested.

"This is gonna spread like wildfire," Cat predicted.

Millie was beginning to regret telling the captain "yes." No one would dare breathe a word to him, but Millie? She would take some heat, no doubt. She frowned.

Annette patted her back. "Don't worry. It'll blow over once the next big thing comes along, which will probably be the arrest of whoever poisoned the staff," she predicted.

"I hope so," Millie muttered.

The girls headed down the stairs to the crew quarters. It had been a long day and judging by what was in store for them tomorrow, they would need to get a good night's rest!

Chapter 24

Andy and Millie waved and smiled at the departing guests until Millie's arm ached and her lips cracked. The morning crawled along and she kept staring at the clock, which hadn't escaped Andy.

When the crowd thinned, he leaned close to Millie. "You're free to go. Have fun." He winked.

Millie groaned. *What had she gotten herself into?*

She made a quick trip to her cabin to change out of her work outfit and slip into a bathing suit, a pair of shorts and t-shirt. She made one final check of her appearance and headed back to the gangway. She didn't even have time to start sweating. Captain Armati stood next to Andy and the two chatted as they watched her approach.

Millie almost didn't recognize Captain Armati out of uniform. He was wearing a pair of turquoise swim trunks and a crisp white t-shirt.

Taut muscles stretched the sleeves of his shirt and rippled from his elbows to the tops of his arms. Millie wondered what he looked like without a shirt and her cheeks turned crimson. *What in the world was she thinking?*

He picked up a backpack lying next to his feet and flung it over his shoulder. "Ready?"

Millie frowned. "Do I need to bring anything?" *Duh! Towels, sunscreen.*

All she had with her was her lanyard and sunglasses.

He shook his head. "Nope, I have towels, bottled water, some sunscreen and insect repellant."

Millie felt foolish but didn't have time to dwell on it. She followed him down the gangway and off the ship.

Two uniformed officers flanked the ramp and lifted a hand in salute as they exited.

Just outside the gates, a car waited. The driver stood on the side of the curb. The captain motioned her to the back seat. Millie climbed in and Captain Armati slid in beside her.

The driver shut the door behind them and made his way to the driver's side.

Although Millie was nervous, the captain put her at ease with stories of his last climb up the falls with his daughter, Fiona, who had visited a few months earlier.

She was surprised at how much Nic, as he insisted she call him now that they were off the ship, knew about the island. She could tell by the way he talked that he enjoyed the diverse culture and the lush, tropical island.

The driver pulled up in front of what looked like a park and they climbed out of the back.

"What time shall I return?" the driver inquired.

"Two hours should be plenty," Nic answered.

They watched as the driver sped off and then wandered down the sidewalk.

Millie heard the falls before she saw them. The closer they got, the louder the roar of the water grew. Still, even with the thunderous sound, she wasn't prepared for the view when they stepped around the corner.

She gasped at the sight of the towering falls. Water cascaded over huge boulders. Millie shaded her eyes and gazed up. She couldn't see the top.

Nic unzipped his backpack and pulled out a small camera. Just then, a couple walked by and Nic asked the man if he would take their picture.

Nic and Millie shuffled over to the railing and angled their bodies so that the falls were directly behind them. Nic eased in next to Millie, casually dropped an arm across her shoulder and smiled for the camera.

Millie thought she was going to have a heart attack. A wave of heat, starting at the top of her head and racing to her toes, rushed over her.

She hadn't been this close to a man, not counting her son, since Roger had left her.

After the young couple snapped the picture, Nic lifted his arm from around Millie, grabbed the camera and shoved it back in his bag.

He took the look of panic on her face to be her worrying about his camera. "Don't worry, the camera is waterproof."

Little did he know...

A large group of climbers ahead of them started to ascend. Nic and Millie waited until the group had reached a higher tier before they started their climb.

He reached back to grab her hand and the two of them waded into the water and sloshed over to the first large boulder.

It was tricky and Millie was glad Nic had told her to bring water shoes. The rocks, covered in thick, green moss, were slippery in spots and a couple times Millie started to lose her balance. Nick was there to keep her steady and before she knew it, they had reached the top.

The views from the top were magnificent and the two of them wandered around for several long moments.

Millie gazed down at the base of the falls. She wondered if they would have to go down the same way they came up.

Nic seemed to have read her mind. "We take the stairs down."

As much as Millie had enjoyed the climb, she was relieved they were taking the easy way down.

They descended the steps, which ended in a flat, grassy area. Lined along the sidewalks were rows of vendors, hawking their wares. They meandered along the tables as they checked out the trinkets and handcrafted souvenirs.

Soon, it was time to leave. From where they were standing, Millie could see the now-familiar car and driver waiting at the curb.

Nic casually reached for Millie's hand and they strolled over to the car. He waited for Millie to climb in the back seat before he slid in next to her.

"Where to?" The driver peered at them through the rearview mirror.

"Scotchie's please."

The car pulled away from the curb and turned left at the stop sign as they drove deep into the jungle.

The paved road turned to a rutted, narrow path. Millie stared out the window at the dense forest as the car jostled along.

Finally, the car pulled up in front of a building that reminded Millie of a shack.

Peeking out behind a thick row of bushes was a covered pavilion with a shiny, tin roof. A small sign hung from the metal overhang. *Scotchies.*

The driver promised to come back later and the two of them wandered through the entrance to the back.

The obscure pavilion masked what lie ahead: a bustling, edge-of-the-jungle, open air restaurant.

On the far side of the room was a long bamboo railing that overlooked a tranquil lagoon. Tiki torches stood sentinel along the rail and Millie decided the place would look either super cool – or super creepy - after dark.

Millie's eye wandered to the ceiling. A thick thatched roof covered the entire restaurant, opening to an outdoor seating area that faced the water. Large, leafy paddle fans hung from the ceiling and helped move the dense, tropical air.

A wooden bar in the center of the restaurant took up a good deal of space while tables fashioned from local driftwood dotted the perimeter.

Carved tiki heads adorned the exterior of the bar and the eyes seemed to focus on Millie. She shivered despite the warm, humid air.

Nic led Millie to a table off in the corner. The menu, already on the table, was simple: pork, chicken and fish. Nic pointed at the menu. "The fish is excellent."

"Sounds good," she declared.

A waiter suddenly appeared. "Good afternoon, man. Are you ready to order?"

"We'll take two virgin zombies." Nic turned to Millie. "Minus the alcohol but I think you'll like it."

The waiter left and Nic changed the subject. "What did you think of the falls?"

"That I've never seen anything like that in my life," she answered truthfully. "You said you brought your daughter here?"

The server returned with the drinks. Millie plucked the turquoise umbrella from the top and sipped the tangerine-colored beverage. It was delicious: a combination of pineapple, orange and something Millie could not quite place.

Nic nodded. "Yes, it was a fun day. Just like today."

Millie set her drink on the table. "Thank you for inviting me. I wouldn't have done this on my own."

The conversation flowed as they talked about children, grandchildren, even the recent storm.

Before Millie knew it, the waiter returned with their meal. Nic was spot on with his suggestion. The fish was delicious and arrived wrapped in a thin layer of tinfoil. The flavor was smoky, the fish moist. It came with a side of rice. Millie had had her fill of rice on the ship but didn't want to hurt Nic's feelings so she ate part of it and left the rest.

They finished their leisurely lunch and Nic glanced down at his watch. "We better head back. The driver is probably waiting."

Millie was sad that the day had gone by so quickly, but he was right and the driver was waiting at the curb when they stepped out of the pavilion.

The drive back to the ship, down the side of the mountain was harrowing with its hairpin turns and blind corners. Several times, Millie was certain they would sideswipe the vehicles headed in the opposite direction and she squeezed her eyes shut.

Halfway down the narrow road, Nic abruptly asked the driver to stop. "Pull over here."

The driver careened off the road and onto a bumpy, dirt drive. Behind a clump of trees was a church: the exterior old and weathered. What had once been a white façade, was now faded from decades of direct sun. Several sections of the brick and stone had turned black.

A large, two-story steeple caught Millie's eye. Near the peak of the steeple was a round clock, tucked into the bricks. The entrance, a cathedral arch and solid wooden door with stained glass in the peak, welcomed visitors.

Nic grabbed the door handle. "I hope you don't mind the detour," he said.

Millie thought the old church was beautiful. She hoped they would be able to venture inside.

"We'll be right back," he told the driver.

Nic climbed out of the car and reached back inside for Millie's hand.

Captain Armati seemed to know where he was going as he made his way along the broken concrete sidewalk. Unkempt weeds had grown between bits of jagged concrete. Wild flowers crept up the side of the stone walls and seemed to peer inside the glass windows.

Nic opened the front door and stepped inside. The interior was cool and dark. They walked silently across the uneven tile floor as they made their way into the sanctuary.

Long rows of worn, wooden pews lined both sides of the aisle. A cross-hung front and center in the sanctuary and a glass podium sat on the stage. The modern podium looked out of place in the beautiful, old church.

When they reached the front, Millie paused. She could feel God's presence. Millie bowed her head. "Thank you, Lord, for bringing me here to this beautiful place of worship." She prayed for several long moments as she soaked in the peacefulness and His presence.

Nic wandered off to the side and waited for Millie to join him.

From somewhere behind them, a male voice, thick with accent echoed. "Captain Armati!"

Millie caught a glimpse of a man dressed in a long, black robe and white sash.

Nic spun around. He met the man halfway, hand extended in greeting. The man of the cloth grabbed Nic's hand and pulled him close.

He released his grip and turned to Millie. "You brought a friend."

Nick held out his hand. "This is Millie. She works on the ship."

The man enveloped her small hand between his two large ones. "I'm so pleased to meet you. Welcome to Tabernacle Church."

"Reverend Miller is an old friend of mine," Nic explained.

The reverend nodded. "Ah, yes. Captain Armati and I go back a long ways. He is a good man," he added.

Nic motioned to the front door. "We can't stay. The car is waiting." Nic reached inside his backpack and pulled out a Zip-loc bag. Inside the bag was an envelope. He handed it to Revered Miller. "This is for you."

The reverend took the envelope then turned it over in his hand. "The Lord will continue to bless you. Thank you for your generosity to our church and congregation."

The two talked for a couple more minutes before Nic and Millie made their way out. Millie waited as Nic quietly closed the door behind them. "Thank you for sharing that with me. It was lovely."

Millie followed Nic out. She focused her attention on the broken sidewalk in front of her, careful not to trip over the corners that jutted up.

Suddenly, Nic grabbed her hand. "We have to go! Now!"

Nic yanked her forward so abruptly Millie lost her footing. She quickly regained her balance and her eyes scanned the street in front of them.

Not far from the church was a small band of men. They were running towards the car – and them!

Millie had a feeling it wasn't the welcome wagon.

Nic and Millie raced toward the car, its engine running.

The driver began to honk the car horn and wave frantically.

Nic flung the back door open and shoved Millie inside. He dove in right after her and then reached back to pull the door shut.

In one swift movement, he unzipped the front pocket of his backpack and pulled out a silver handgun.

The men had reached the side of the car. They began to pound on the passenger window with jagged rocks. *Bam! Bam!*

Nic lifted the gun and pointed it at the window.

The men caught a glimpse of the gun in Nic's hand and took a step back.

Seeing their chance to escape, the driver rammed the shifter into reverse and peeled out of the church parking lot.

The men chased after the car. One of them managed to fling himself onto the trunk of the car. His face contorted in a fit of rage.

Millie couldn't hear what he was saying but judging by the look on his face, she was glad that he was on the other side of the glass!

The driver's eyes darted to the rearview mirror. "It's time to lose him."

He jerked the steering wheel to the right, sending the car careening sideways.

The unwanted hitchhiker slid to the side, his fingers clawing at the small lip that separated the trunk from the car frame. Still, he hung on.

The driver jerked the wheel the other way.

Finally, the man shot across the smooth surface and fell to the gravel road below.

Apparently unharmed by the fall, he jumped to his feet, lifted both of his hands and shook his middle finger at them.

Millie turned to face Nic, who calmly placed his weapon into the front pocket of his backpack. "Y-you..." She didn't know where to start.

Nic finished her sentence. "Can never be too cautious." He reached forward and patted the driver's shoulder. "Way to go, Navaro."

Navaro wiped his hand across his forehead. "Close call, that time, boss."

Back at the port, Millie stood on the edge of the curb and waited while Nic paid Navaro, then followed him through security and up the gangplank.

Millie realized she had just enough time to shower and change before she had to meet Andy back at the entrance to greet guests as they boarded.

Before she left, she thanked Nic, Captain Armati now that they were back on the ship, for a lovely day.

"I'm sorry about what just happened," he apologized.

Millie held up her hand. "No need to apologize. You saved our lives."

For a brief moment, their eyes met and Millie had the crazy thought that he might lean over and kiss her, but then she realized that would not happen. Too many eyes were watching.

Instead, he smiled, bowed and then stepped onto the elevator while Millie crossed the lobby and opened the door that led to the crew quarters. They lived in two different worlds, the captain and Millie. She wondered if maybe those worlds were too big of a bridge to gap.

Inside the cabin, Millie stripped off her clothes and turned the shower knobs to a lukewarm temperature. The water felt wonderful. Millie washed the sweat from her body and scrubbed her hair with her favorite jasmine scented shampoo.

She towel-dried her hair and pulled it back in a tight bun before she slipped into her work uniform and stepped out of the small space.

Sarah was sitting at the desk. The two rarely ran into each other in the cabin. They were like two ships passing in the night for the most part.

Millie could tell Sarah had gone ashore too. Her young friend was wearing a pair of shorts and sleeveless blouse. She stood as Millie headed to her closet.

"I saw you at the falls." Sarah smiled.

"And?"

"You are the talk of the ship," Sarah said. "Not in a bad way, though. Everyone thinks it's cute."

Cute? She and Captain Armati were cute? Millie groaned. It could be worse. Maybe.

Millie got more of the same when she met Andy at the gangway. "You look relaxed."

"It was fun," Millie answered.

"I've never been to the falls," Andy said, "or Scotchies," he added.

Millie slapped her forehead with the palm of her hand. "Is there anyone that doesn't know what I did today?"

Andy gazed up, as if seriously considering the question. He shook his head. "Maybe Captain Vitale."

He left her alone after that, as hordes of passengers descended on the ship. They spent the next several hours welcoming the guest back onboard. Several stopped by to tell Millie they had seen her at the falls. *Great! Now even the passengers knew!*

Finally, the last guest wandered up the ramp and the crew pulled the door closed. Millie knew the drill. She had just enough time to grab a quick bite to eat, although she still wasn't hungry after eating the fish and rice.

Instead, she headed up to the lido deck for the sail away party. It was in full swing and the guests were having a ball.

Billows of smoke poured out of the smokestack behind Millie as the ship charged full steam ahead toward South Seas Cay. Millie stayed long enough to watch the island disappear from sight. She wondered if Captain Armati – Nic – was watching it, too.

She turned to go, her mind already switching gears. The countdown had officially begun. Soon, Cat, Annette and Millie would put their plan in action!

Chapter 25

Annette and her kitchen staff had gathered in the galley. Next to Annette, in the center of the large prep table, was a rich, burgundy tablecloth.

Annette clasped her hands together. Her eyes brightened as she addressed her captive audience. "I can't wait to share with you my latest creations."

She reached out and with one dramatic swoop, yanked the cloth. Under the cloth were several sets of elegant platters.

Annette bypassed the small platters as she reached for a large, oval platter loaded with the treats. She picked up the tray and passed it around, encouraging everyone to take one of the decadent desserts that filled the tray.

Each crewmember took one of the treats and passed the dish to the next person. They all agreed they were delicious.

"These special dishes right here are on their way to the officers," she explained. "I need some volunteers to help deliver them."

Almost all of the kitchen staff raised their hands. This was a coveted assignment. Any time a crew had a chance to serve one of the officers was a good thing.

Annette hand selected the deliverers, starting with Captain Armati and working her way down the line. When she got to Donovan Sweeney, she chose Veronica Chang. Noel Kalani would deliver Detective Patterson's surprise.

Everything was falling into place.

She glanced at her watch. "Ten minutes from now, we will begin delivery," she announced.

Annette slipped on her sunglasses. That would give the culprit just enough time to do their dastardly deed and she would be watching!

***

The plan was in place: Cat would follow Noel. Millie would tail Veronica.

Annette had tipped off both Donovan and Patterson, warning them not to take even a single bite of the tempting goodies.

Millie hid just inside the entrance to "Formals," the tuxedo shop, and behind a mannequin that sported a navy blue tuxedo. She had an unobstructed view of the kitchen door and could easily slip behind Veronica as she made her way to Donovan's office.

Along the path was a small, side corridor rarely used by staff. It would be the perfect spot for Veronica to slip inside and poison the sweets.

Cat was waiting for Noel on the other side of the kitchen. Noel would head in the opposite direction, towards Patterson's office on a lower level. Her task to trail Noel would be a bit trickier since there were a lot more stop off points where Noel could poison the food. Cat would have to be on her toes!

Cat tipped her foot to the side and gazed at her black velvet stilettos. They weren't the best shoes to wear when in stealth-mode. *What on earth had she been thinking?*

Millie had problems of her own. She wondered what their next step would be if this mission failed!

She glanced down at her watch. Any second now...

At precisely 5:15 p.m., Veronica stepped out of the kitchen and strolled past *Formals*. Millie silently slipped in behind her, careful to keep her distance.

Veronica meandered along. She stopped in front of the mirror, which was just inside the display case of the jewelry shop, and fiddled with her hair.

Satisfied each silky lock was in place, she continued walking. Veronica slowed when she got to the side corridor. Millie slowed and turned so her back faced Veronica as she pretended to look out the window. She could see Veronica's reflection in the glass.

Veronica had reached the upper level of the atrium, just steps from Donovan's office. She paused for a moment, then pushed the half door open and stepped behind the guest services counter, sans a dish of poisonous goodies.

***

Cat peeked from behind the exit door. Noel, with a bounce in her step, carried her covered dish through the hall, humming as she walked.

She waved at each person she passed. After about the fifth pass-by and her sickeningly sweet greeting, Cat wanted to throw up. *Could anyone really be that nice?*

Noel descended the side steps and stopped on Deck 2 where she turned in. The area was deserted.

302

Cat tiptoed down the steps. The heel of her shoe caught on a corner of loose carpet and stair tread.

Cat jerked her foot. Her troublesome shoe refused to budge and she started to lose her balance.

She teetered back and forth, one arm holding the rail in a death grip. Her other arm flailed in circles like a windmill on steroids.

Cat finally regained her balance and pulled again – harder this time.

The carpet ripped, releasing Cat's shoe and she started to tumble down the step. *Thump! Thump!*

Cat reached out and wrapped both arms around the railing, desperate to halt her free fall.

Noel turned back at the sound. She tilted her head and looked up.

Cat flattened her body and lowered her head. She sucked in a breath, squeezed her eyes shut and prayed Noel hadn't seen her.

Noel shrugged and continued to walk.

When she reached the entrance door that separated the crew quarters from the guest area, she stopped.

Noel's eyes scanned the small hall, starting on the left and travelling all the way over to the right.

Convinced that there was no one around, she lifted the lid of the tray and tucked the cover under her right arm. Next, she delicately lifted one of the chocolate covered morsels and popped it into her mouth before sliding the rest of the pieces around on the plate to fill the empty gap.

Noel finished her walk down the long corridor.

Cat peeked around the corner and watched as the door to Patterson's office opened and Noel stepped inside.

Cat leaned her forehead against the metal door. If Noel was the saboteur, she had not poisoned that batch!

***

"Millie! Do you copy?"

Millie unclipped her radio and lifted it to her lips. Her eyes never left the guest services desk as she waited for Veronica to emerge from Donovan's office.

"I'm here. Perp number one is inside Donovan's office."

"You need to get in there. I've been trying to call Donovan on his radio and office phone and there's no answer. You need to make sure he doesn't eat those desserts!"

"So we have a positive ID?"

"We do and it's not who you think," Annette answered. "Look, I gotta go. I need the tray back as evidence."

"10-4. I'll retrieve the goods and return stat." Millie clipped the walkie-talkie to her belt and hustled down the steps. She pushed the half door and made her way to the back.

Zane Gretski lifted a hand, as if to stop her.

Millie wasn't in the mood. Not right now. "Don't bother!" she warned him.

Millie tapped on Donovan's door and waited - no answer. She knocked a second time – louder this time.

"Come in," Donovan's muffled voice echoed through the door.

Millie sucked in a breath, grabbed the door handle and pushed it open.

Her eyes went right to the silver tray in the center of Donovan's desk. She let out a sigh of relief when she noticed the lid was still in place.

Veronica's eyes narrowed when she saw Millie. She rose from her chair, directly across from Donovan. "I should get back to the kitchen." She nodded at Donovan, ignored Millie and flounced out of the room, irritated that Millie had interrupted.

Millie watched her leave and shrugged. "Good riddance."

She nodded to the dish. "You didn't eat…"

"Nope. You told me not to," he pointed out.

She reached for the tray. "It was for a good reason. Annette just radioed." Her eyes narrowed. "She's been trying to call you."

Donovan reached for his radio, sitting on the edge of his desk. "Huh. It's off." He clicked the button to turn it back on.

"Anyways, she said I needed to bring these back. They're evidence."

Donovan leaned back in his chair. "Veronica?"

Millie shook her head. "I'm not sure. Annette said it wasn't who we thought." Which would mean it wasn't Veronica – or Noel. But if it wasn't those two, who was it?

Alison had seen a woman who fit Veronica or Noel's description leave the poisoned coffee on Andy's desk.

Millie picked up the tray and headed for the door. She was about to find out.

Chapter 26

A small group had gathered in the galley. Annette, Amit, Raj, Cat, Veronica, Noel and Dave Patterson, along with a uniformed officer who stood off to one side, blocking the exit.

Annette looked up when Millie stepped into the kitchen. "Good. You're just in time."

Millie set the covered tray on the gleaming counter and pushed it towards Annette.

Annette pulled the tray in front of her. "These desserts have been poisoned." She lifted her finger and pointed at Raj. "Raj did it."

The color drained from Raj's face. "I-I..."

Annette waved a dismissive hand. "Don't bother. I caught you red-handed, squirting droplets of liquid on these." Her eyes dropped to the front pocket of his jacket. "Empty your pockets."

Raj crossed his arms and straightened his back. "What if I refuse?" he challenged.

Dave Patterson and the officer took a step forward. "It would be in your best interest to do as you were told," Patterson said in a low voice.

Raj slowly reached inside his pocket and pulled out the contents: a tube of ChapStick, 3 breath mints and a small, clear bottle with a pale green liquid inside.

Patterson grabbed the bottle and held it up. "Is this the bottle?" he asked Annette.

"Yes, it is."

Patterson turned to Raj. "This is a serious matter - attempted murder. You could have killed someone. You almost killed Captain Vitale."

While Patterson addressed Raj, Millie studied the faces of the small group. They all looked shocked. Everyone that is, except for Noel Kalani. Sweet, little Noel looked terrified. She licked her lips and stared at Raj, her eyes never leaving his face.

Raj had applied for Annette's job. Millie remembered seeing his application. He had motive and opportunity, but something was missing...

The officer stepped forward and grasped Raj's wrist.

"Wait!" Millie blurted out.

All eyes turned to Millie.

Millie eased through the crowd and came up next to Noel.

"What's going on here, Noel? Do you know something about the poisonings?" Millie probed.

Noel's eyes grew as round as saucers. She began to shake her head. "N-no. I-I'm as shocked as you," she said.

Millie tried a different tactic. She nodded her head towards Raj. "Raj really likes you."

"Yes." Noel nodded.

"Amit, too."

"Hmm," Noel agreed.

"Raj, Amit and you. All three of you submitted applications for Annette's job but not Veronica."

A mask dropped over Noel's sweet face. Her eyes glittered with anger. "She didn't deserve the job."

The remark ticked Veronica off. She stomped across the room and stuck her face in Noel's face. "Why not?" she demanded.

"Because all you can do is flirt and bat your eyes." Noel imitated Veronica's eye batting to a "T." Despite the seriousness of the situation, Millie covered the grin that spread across her face.

"So I don't deserve the job, although I am as qualified, if not better qualified than you are. On top of that, I'm prettier," Veronica spat out.

"I don't think so." Noel rolled her eyes before continuing. "I never told Raj to poison anyone. He did that on his own."

"But you knew about it." Annette was incredulous.

Noel shrugged. "I had my suspicions."

The pieces were falling into place.

Millie leaned forward. "So you hinted to Raj that if you got Annette out of the way, you could take her job." Millie wondered what would possess someone to hurt others over a stupid job!

Cat picked up where Millie left off. "You couldn't stand Veronica so you made sure she was the one to deliver the poisoned coffee and food and take the rap. Annette would be out of the picture, Veronica would be in jail and you would have your dream job."

Whack! Veronica slapped Noel across the face.

Noel, in retaliation, grabbed a handful of Veronica's hair and the two women began punching each other.

Patterson and the officer quickly broke up the fight but not before they got a couple sharp, gut punches in.

"Noel Kalani and Raj Soo Ang, you are both under arrest for attempted murder." Patterson said.

The group watched in stunned silence as Patterson led Noel and Raj out of the kitchen.

Poor Amit stood silently watching, his mouth gaping in shock. Millie was glad Amit hadn't been involved for Annette's sake. He was a good guy and Annette considered him a friend.

Cat shoved a hand on her hip. "Well, doesn't that just take the cake."

After the dust settled, the crowd dispersed, which left only Cat, Annette and Millie.

Millie was curious. "The glasses worked."

Annette reached inside her pocket and pulled them out. "Like a charm."

If not for Annette's brilliant idea, the blame would have fallen squarely on Veronica Chang's innocent shoulders. Millie wasn't Veronica's biggest fan. One never knew about people. If she put the two women side-by-side with what little she knew, she would have picked Veronica as the culprit all day long. This was a good lesson for Millie: never judge a book, or in this case, a person, by the cover.

The dinner rush would soon be in full swing. Cat needed to return to the store, Millie to check in with Andy and to start her evening routine.

Guests had started to congregate outside the theater for the Captain's Cocktail Party. It was a fun event for past guests, full of food and free drinks, which was always a hit. The place was packed.

She stopped by guest services to chat with Donovan for a moment. He had escaped his poisoning, thanks to the girls and she wanted his take on their discovery.

He was on the office phone when she wandered inside. He waved her to the seat. "Yes, sir. I'll take care of that and I agree with you one hundred percent. We have the best crew on board Siren of the Seas."

He hung up the phone and grinned at Millie. "Just the person I was looking for." Donovan opened his right hand desk drawer, reached inside and pulled out Millie's keycard – the one that gave her access to almost all areas of the ship. It was the card he'd taken from Millie when they discovered she'd used it to sneak into his office.

"You can have this back." He slid it across the table. "You earned it."

Not one to look a gift horse in the mouth, Millie pulled the temporary lanyard from around her neck and slipped her permanent one on. "Sweet. Thank you."

The two chatted for several moments before Millie glanced down at her watch. She needed to get backstage to prep for the main show.

Millie stood.

Donovan held out a hand. "Oh! I've been hanging onto this pile of mail for a couple days now. There is something in here for you and a couple pieces of mail for Cat. Do you mind dropping this off on your way to the theater?"

"No problem." Millie grabbed the mail and made her way out the door. She had just enough time to drop Cat's mail on her way.

Millie flipped through the small stack as she walked. There was a letter from her cousin, Gloria. She folded the envelope in half and shoved it into her front pocket.

The other two pieces were addressed to Cat. One of them looked like a letter from a court and the other piece of mail, addressed to Cat, had been handwritten, her name scrawled carelessly across the front. The ship's name and address below it.

She lifted her eyes to the top left hand corner. There was no return address: just one word, one name – Jay.

The end.

The series continues...Look for Book #4, to released October 2015.

Visit my website for new releases and special offers: **www.hopecallaghan.com**

Lobster Bisque

Ingredients:

1 cup chicken broth
1/4 cup diced yellow or red onion
4 tablespoons butter
4 tablespoons all-purpose flour
1 cup whole milk (or substitute w/reduced fat milk)
1 cup heavy cream
1/2 teaspoon salt
1/2 teaspoon pepper
2 tablespoons tomato puree (optional – for color)
1/2 teaspoon garlic powder
1 pound cooked and cubed lobster meat
1 teaspoon Worcestershire sauce
1 pinch ground cayenne pepper

Directions:

In a small frying pan place 1/4 cup chicken broth and the onion. Cook over a low heat for 5 to 7 minutes.

In a medium size pot over medium heat melt the butter. Slowly whisk in flour. Whisk until a creamy mixture is blended.

Gradually pour in remainder of chicken broth, whisking constantly.

319

Whisk in milk, heavy cream, salt, pepper, onion, garlic powder, lobster meat, Worcestershire sauce, cayenne pepper, tomato puree (optional).

Simmer soup for one hour

About The Author

Hope Callaghan is an author who loves to write Christian books, especially Christian Mystery and Cozy Mystery books. Born and raised in a small town in West Michigan, she now lives in Florida with her husband.

She is the proud mother of one daughter and a stepdaughter and stepson. When she's not doing the thing she loves best - writing books - she enjoys cooking, traveling and reading books.

Hope loves to connect with her readers!

Visit **hopecallaghan.com** for information on special offers and soon-to-be-released books!

Email: hope@hopecallaghan.com

Facebook page:
http://www.facebook.com/hopecallaghanauthor

Other Books by Author, Hope Callaghan:

DECEPTION CHRISTIAN MYSTERY SERIES:

Waves of Deception: Samantha Rite Series Book 1
Winds of Deception: Samantha Rite Series Book 2
Tides of Deception: Samantha Rite Series Book 3

GARDEN GIRLS CHRISTIAN COZY MYSTERIES SERIES:

Who Murdered Mr. Malone? Garden Girls Mystery Series Book 1
Grandkids Gone Wild: Garden Girls Mystery Series Book 2
Smoky Mountain Mystery: Garden Girls Mystery Series Book 3
Death by Dumplings: Garden Girls Mystery Series Book 4
Eye Spy: Garden Girls Mystery Series Book 5

Magnolia Mansion Mysteries: Garden Girls Mystery Series Book 6
Missing Milt: Garden Girls Mystery Series Book 7
Garden Girls Christian Cozy Mysteries Boxed Set Books 1-3

CRUISE SHIP CHRISTIAN COZY MYSTERIES SERIES:

Starboard Secrets Cruise Ship Cozy Mysteries Book 1
Portside Peril: Cruise Ship Cozy Mysteries Book 2

Made in United States
North Haven, CT
03 June 2024

53257413R00200